AUTHOR   CLASS

BRUCE, L.   M

TITLE

Jack on the gallows tree

Jack on the Gallows Tree

WITHIN the space of an hour or two the dead bodies of two elderly ladies, Miss Sophia Carew and Mrs. Westmacott, were discovered in the vicinity of the town of Buddington-on-the-Hill; both women had been very recently murdered; death in each case had been caused by strangulation; each was found lying at full length clasping in her hands the stem of a Madonna lily. As far as anyone knew there was no connection between the two women; they had never met each other; although both were well-to-do there was no evidence that a beneficiary from the will of one could expect any benefit from the will of the other.

The work of a maniac? Could there be two murderers planning together their foul deeds? It falls to Carolus Deene, the inimitable schoolmaster—who was supposed to be taking it easy, recuperating from a severe attack of jaundice—to unravel the knot of mystery and prove himself once again a master detective.

Also by Leo Bruce

THE 'SERGEANT BEEF' SERIES

Jack on the Gallows Tree

By
LEO BRUCE

IAN HENRY PUBLICATIONS
1980

03473033

Copyright © 1960 Propertius Company Ltd.

First published by Peter Davies Ltd.

This edition, 1980

ISBN 0 86025 158 6

Made and printed in Great Britain by
R. J. Acford, Industrial Estate, Chichester, Sussex
for Ian Henry Publications Ltd.,
38 Parkstone Avenue, Hornchurch, Essex, RM11 3LW

For three wild lads were we, brave boys,
And three wild lads were we;
Thou on the land, and I on the sand,
And Jack on the gallows tree!

SIR WALTER SCOTT
Guy Mannering

1

"*Torquay Deaths: Man Questioned*," read out Mr Gorringer in a voice stern with disapproval.

"Drink your tea before it's cold, dear," said his wife. "I don't know what you're worrying about. There's always something in the papers."

Mr Gorringer, headmaster of the Queen's School, Newminster, cleared his throat with an enduring and significant rumble.

"In the circumstances, my dear, I have every cause to worry. Every cause. All the acts of violence this morning seem to have taken place at seaside resorts."

"Well?" said Mrs Gorringer, whom her husband considered a witty woman, though not, fortunately, at breakfast time.

"You are doubtless aware that my Senior History Master, Carolus Deene, is being sent by his medical adviser for a period of recuperation by the sea after a severe illness. Hm. *Bournemouth Model Found Dead. Police Search for Man with Arm in Plaster*. It's a serious matter."

"But surely, if Carolus is recovering from jaundice he won't have time or energy to get mixed up in anything of that sort?"

Mr Gorringer set down his large teacup.

"In some years of experience of Deene, my dear, I have never known him in any circumstances to lack the energy or the time for his sordid hobby. If he finds himself within reach of a corpse—I speak figuratively, of course—he will become involved in details which are most unfitting in an assistant of mine here at Newminster. If he catches so much as a whiff of murder he will be on the scent with all the persistence and gusto of a dachshund in search of truffles."

"Do dachshunds search for truffles?"

"I have always understood so. It explains their extraordinary shape, no doubt. Can you wonder at my anxiety? *Scarborough Case: Woman Charged*. It's nothing short of disturbing."

"Oh, I don't know," said Mrs Gorringer. "I don't see it does much harm. It's a hobby, like any other. It seems to bring the school's name forward, if anything."

Mr Gorringer addressed his wife as though she were the Board of Governors.

"I do not fail to realize that Deene's book *Who Killed William Rufus? And Other Mysteries of History* enjoyed considerable popularity among readers of a certain class," he said. "I am perfectly aware that his reputation extends beyond the confines of our academic backwater. I recognize that as a teacher he is both talented and assiduous. But I cannot for a moment accept the fact that these excursions of his into contemporary crime do anything but besmirch the fair name of the Queen's School. It has come to my ears that even while on his sickbed in the school sanatorium he was engaged in reading a work called *The Etiology of Delinquent and Criminal Behaviour* by an American writer no doubt suitably named Walter C. Reckless. What am I to say to that? Now that he is to be sent to the seaside, I feel something very like alarm."

"Why not get Dr Tom to suggest somewhere else? A resort in which they don't murder one another?"

"It is not so easy as you imagine, my dear. These unfortunate cases seem positively to follow Deene. However, I will as you suggest have a word with Dr Thomas. It may be some retreat can be found from which Deene will find it hard to escape."

Mr Gorringer rose and set his mortarboard firmly on

8

his head so that his large red ears protruded over the lower part of it. He pulled on his gown and in a short while was crossing the school quadrangle at a swinging yet dignified pace.

On reaching his study he rang for the school porter, a disgruntled individual called Muggeridge, who resented his orders to wear a uniform that included a gold-braided silk hat.

"Yes?" sighed Muggeridge when he appeared.

Mr Gorringer ignored this.

"Good morning, Muggeridge," he said brightly but firmly. "I want a word with Dr Thomas."

"He's not here."

"I am perfectly aware that Dr Thomas does not come to the school until eleven o'clock, Muggeridge. When he pays his call be so good as to ask him to see me, please."

"If I can catch him I will. He dives in and out like a jack-in-the-box sometimes."

"Just make a point of it," said Mr Gorringer loftily.

The porter turned to go.

"Oh, by the way, Muggeridge. There is something I have frequently intended to ask you. What is your Christian name?"

"Mal . . ." began the porter.

"Don't say it!" said Mr Gorringer in some alarm.

"Malachi, if you want to know. It's not my fault and I told my father about it years ago. Saddling anyone with . . ."

"That will do, thank you, Muggeridge. You may go."

At eleven o'clock the headmaster was again seated at his large desk, apparently absorbed in the papers before him. When the doctor entered he looked up and spoke affably.

"Ah, Thomas," he said. "I wanted a word with you. Pray take a seat. How is our friend Deene?"

"He's all right," said the doctor carelessly. "I'm packing him off in a day or two for a fortnight's sea air."

"It was that which I wished to discuss with you. After his unfortunate illness he is doubtless in a somewhat weak condition?"

"Oh, Carolus has a tough constitution. He will be fit as a flea in a week or ten days."

"By which time our term will be finished. Where did you think of recommending him to go?"

"It doesn't matter much, really, so long as he gets some good air. Torquay, perhaps. Scarborough. Bournemouth. Wherever he likes."

The headmaster winced.

"I cannot help but feel," he said, "that he would be better suited by one of the inland spas."

"Oh. Why?"

"You are perhaps aware of his predilection for involving himself in criminology? It would surely be disastrous to his health if at this time when he so sorely needs rest he were to be brought in contact with something which would disturb his repose and retard his recovery?"

Dr Thomas smiled.

"I don't know. He likes that sort of thing. It might do him a power of good."

"There is another aspect of the matter," said Mr Gorringer. "I have the good name of the school to remember. Our coastal resorts seem just now to provide an abundance of such cases as we wish Deene to avoid. Can we not conspire to suggest Malvern perhaps? Tunbridge Wells? Cheltenham Spa? Harrogate? They seem pleasantly free from the deeds of violence by which our patient is attracted."

"I daresay an inland resort would be just as good for him," admitted the doctor. "I could send him to Buddington-on-the-Hill, if you like."

"I should be immensely obliged," said the headmaster. "Immensely. It is, I believe, a quiet little town in peaceful surroundings."

"All right," said Dr Thomas, rising. "I'll tell him. There's a passable hotel there."

"Do you not think a nursing home might be preferable?"

"It might, but Carolus wouldn't stay in it. I must run. I'll do what I can."

But this did not altogether reassure the headmaster. He was noticeably thoughtful during the morning and when he passed the music master in the cloisters his "Ah, Tubley . . ." seemed positively absent-minded.

Towards the end of the afternoon he again summoned Muggeridge.

"At what time is the evening paper on sale?" he enquired.

"It's out now," said the porter. "But I can tell you what won the two-thirty."

"Do not be impertinent," said Mr Gorringer. "You are perfectly aware that I take no interest in horse-racing. It would ill befit my position."

"I don't know. Some of them do all right," said Muggeridge darkly.

"You are not referring to the staff, I trust?"

"Hollingbourne brought up a double yesterday. But he's not often lucky. Some of the boys study form better than him."

Mr Gorringer controlled himself, for he was anxious to know more.

"Really?" he said with elephantine casualness. "That surprises me."

"It didn't ought to. Young Priggley's a consistent winner. I feel like following him sometimes."

"That will do, thank you, Muggeridge. Now kindly purchase the evening paper, which I need for quite different reasons."

The porter sighed and went out while Mr Gorringer made a note in the small pocket-book he carried. 'See Priggley. Horse-racing', it ominously read.

When his newspaper came he studied it with care. He found that at Torquay, where a family of three had apparently been killed by poisoning, the person previously questioned had now been charged with murder. He was, according to the news-sheet, a wealthy numismatist from Gateshead. At Bournemouth the man with his arm in plaster had been taken to the local police station and was still there 'up to a late hour' last night. The Scarborough case looked even more open-and-shut and 'the woman', a Birmingham housewife, had been remanded in custody.

Mr Gorringer sighed and after glancing at his watch set out for the school sanatorium. His best course, he felt, was to see Carolus Deene for himself and if necessary make a personal appeal. He did not want his anxiety to last throughout the coming Easter holidays, which he planned to spend as usual at the Sandringham Private Hotel at Brighton. He dreamed of a promise from Carolus Deene which would allay his fears.

He found his Senior History Master sitting up in bed reading Lucas's *Forensic Chemistry and Scientific Criminal Investigation*.

Carolus Deene was in his early forties. He had been a good all-round athlete with a half blue for boxing and a fine record in athletics. During the war he did violent things, always with a certain elegance for which he was famous. He jumped out of aeroplanes with a parachute and actually killed a couple of men with his Commando knife which, he supposed ingenuously, had been issued to him for that purpose.

He was slim, dapper, rather pale and he dressed too well for a schoolmaster. He was not a good disciplinarian as the headmaster understood the word because he simply could not be bothered with discipline, being far too interested in his subject. If there were stupid boys who did not feel this interest and preferred to sit at the back of his class and eat revolting sweets he let them, continuing to talk to the few who listened. He was popular, but considered a little odd. His dressiness and passionate interest in both history and crime were his best-known characteristics in the school, though among the staff his large private income was a matter for some invidious comment.

"Ah, Deene," said Mr Gorringer, "making good progress, I see."

"Yes thanks, headmaster. Do find a seat."

"I notice you are doing a little light reading."

"Yes. It's not bad," said Carolus. "Sorry I shan't be able to do my stuff with the exams."

"Truly a pity. But jaundice is jaundice. I hear that Dr Thomas is recommending you to go away for a period of complete rest."

"Sounds as though I'd had a nervous breakdown. Yes, Tom did say he thought I ought to have a change of air."

"Where did you think of going?" asked Mr Gorringer, keeping his voice as casual as possible.

"It doesn't seem to matter. Doctors have given up pretending that one resort is better than another, I gather."

"He did not recommend any particular spa for you?"

"He said something about Buddington-on-the-Hill, I believe. But it sounded deathly dull."

"An excellent choice, my dear Deene. A splendid little place. It would build you up in no time, I feel sure."

"I don't really mind. Tom says there's a reasonably good hotel there."

"I rejoice to hear it. You will no doubt make reservations there forthwith?"

"I suppose so."

Mr Gorringer wished him a quick recovery and left with a lighter heart. When, four days later, he heard that the school doctor had himself driven Carolus to Buddington and returned to say that he was comfortably settled at the Royal Hydro, and would remain there for at least three weeks, the headmaster could read of the deepening mystery at Torquay, the police baffled at Bournemouth, the surprising developments at Scarborough without losing his large appetite.

On the Saturday after the departure of Carolus he decided to take his History Master's place and conduct a lesson with the Lower Sixth, a difficult class dominated by that odiously sophisticated boy, Rupert Priggley. Mr Gorringer found that Carolus had left the class deep in the affairs of the fourteenth century.

For the headmaster history was firmly divided into 'reigns' and he tackled that of Richard II with a will. He found the class curiously attentive as he ran through Richard's wily tactics, his sudden arresting of his opponents and finally his own deposition.

"Parliament ordered that Richard should be imprisoned," pronounced Mr Gorringer sonorously as he secretly wondered how this class had gained a reputation for unruliness. "He was privily removed from the Tower of London and sent to Pontefract Castle. He lived through most of the winter, but in February he died." Mr Gorringer paused to prepare his final peroration.

A boy named Simmons, a studious and bespectacled youth, devoted to study, the headmaster believed, asked a question.

"What did he die of, sir?"

It was innocently spoken.

"History does not record . . ." began Mr Gorringer.

"Wasn't he starved to death, sir?"

"Wasn't it straight murder, sir?"

"Why was his corpse never shown to the people as Parliament ordered, sir?"

"What exactly was the mystery, sir?"

Mr Gorringer looked about him, realizing too late the guile of the innocent-looking Simmons.

"It does not seem to be a point of much historical interest," he said airily. "Privation of one sort or another, no doubt."

"Murder, then?" suggested Priggley.

"Murder, mayhap, neglect, discomfort, illness, starvation. Who is to say?" asked the headmaster rhetorically.

"Mr Deene, if he were here," retorted Priggley. "It would be just his cup of tea. He'd probably run down to Pontefract looking for clues."

"That will do, Priggley. We will now . . ."

"You must own it's most unsatisfactory, sir. Here's a king just petering out, as it were. One should know at least whether he was assassinated."

"When your History Master returns to his duties you will no doubt be able to inveigle him into speculation on that wholly irrelevant point . . ."

"It wouldn't be irrelevant to him, sir. It would be *the* point. Who did it. How. Why. When. Where. Right up his street."

"Silence, sir!" said Mr Gorringer in an intimidating voice. "Let us now consider the character of this sovereign and its effect on contemporary events . . ."

The lesson went on without further interruption and Mr Gorringer was able to dismiss the class with good-humour.

As he was walking home half an hour later he found Priggley in wait for him. In the boy's hand was a copy of the evening paper.

"Seen this, sir?"

Mr Gorringer took the paper and began to scan its headlines. Scarborough. Bournemouth. Torquay. He could look at news items now without dismay.

"By the way, Priggley," he said as his eyes roved. "I have to speak to you on a most serious matter. It has come to my ears that you have . . ." His voice died away and Rupert Priggley was gratified to see his mouth fall open and his eyes goggle.

"Confound it!" cried the headmaster. It was the nearest

15

to an oath that he allowed himself to go in the presence of a pupil.

"Pretty little paragraph, isn't it, sir?"

Words failed Mr Gorringer.

"It's . . . it's . . ." he said and stood staring at the newspaper.

"Rather Mr Deene's tea, don't you think, sir?"

Double Murder at Buddington, Mr Gorringer read. *Two Elderly Ladies Found Strangled.*

He perused the details which Priggley had already seen. Two women, believed to be unacquainted with one another, had been murdered during a single night in or near the town of Buddington-on-the-Hill. The body of a spinster, Miss Sophia Carew, had been discovered some four miles from the town, while that of Mrs Westmacott, a widow with several surviving children, was lying in a sitting-room of her house, Rossetti Lodge. Death had been caused in each case by strangulation.

"This," said Mr Gorringer at last, "this is terrible."

Rupert Priggley, who did not for a moment suppose that he was referring to the violence of the two poor women's death, said quietly, "I was afraid you wouldn't like it, sir."

2

THE mineral springs of Buddington were known to the Romans, and excavations have shown a complicated water system and brought to light the remains of a lead-lined bath and certain mosaics. In the eighteenth century one of the Georges took to coming here, and though it never rivalled

Bath or Tunbridge Wells as a spa, it had its vogue and shows traces of it in its architecture.

Today it is famous for its population of rich and aged invalids and the fact that here, alone in all England, the bath-chair survives as more than a relic. On any fine morning you may see on the wide pavements of the street called the Promenade an almost continuous procession of these man-drawn vehicles, which are hired and pulled by their owners at the standard rate of thirty shillings an hour.

Though the town stands high, it is very much on a level, which makes the work of the bathchair-men easier and enables their patrons to be drawn not only to the famous Pump Room but less hygienically to the Olde Creamerie, where at eleven o'clock in the morning they may be seen swallowing milky coffee and devouring sugared and sickly cakes.

The Royal Hydro Hotel was not, unhappily, built to accommodate the royal visitors of the eighteenth century, but looks rather as though its architect hoped Prince Albert might decide to stay there. Seeing it on a rise above the town, one remembers the Crystal Palace before its destruction, the Albert Hall, St Pancras Station, the Law Courts in the Strand, even the Victoria and Albert Museum. Its horrors are manifold and include the huge conservatory on the side of the building which is full of misplaced tropical verdure.

Carolus arrived feeling thoroughly exhausted by the journey and scarcely glanced about him as he stood in the towering entrance hall among giant pilasters and gilt stucco. He found his room had a rich and stuffy atmosphere in spite of its height; curtains, carpets, bedding, upholstery, cushions—everything was heavy, plushy and expensive. However, he had given instructions that he was not to be disturbed, so he climbed into the bed, which was too soft and clinging, and slept till the morning.

His ring then was answered by a spruce young waiter

whose appearance bore the stamp of the Royal Air Force, but who talked like someone learning to broadcast.

He arranged Carolus's breakfast on a table and handed him a couple of newspapers.

"I thought you'd probably want *The Times*," he said, "but I've brought the local daily as well. There's something in it which may interest you."

"Really?"

"Yes. Rather an unusual double murder. I believe that's your line of country."

"I've come here for a rest," said Carolus feebly.

"I know. But you may as well read it. Anything else you want?"

Carolus shook his head rather listlessly and watched the young waiter depart. He felt painfully devitalized, and while trying to eat his breakfast ignored both newspapers.

But that could not last. At first warily then with avidity he read in the *Buddington Courier* all that could be published of the case, and though he made a feeble effort in the days that followed to avoid it in conversation, he was soon absorbed in its details. Before the first two days of his supposed convalescence were over he had become conversant with the outline of the case, largely through the information of the young waiter, who had been born in Buddington and seemed to know all about the town.

Carolus found the story anomalous, bizarre and rather horrifying. Story? Or stories? That was, he decided from the first, the very heart of the matter. The two deaths must certainly be connected, but by what? It could not be by some fantastic coincidence that there had taken place in the same night and in the same town. But were they the acts of a single person? Or two persons acting in concert? Or independently? These questions came before all else.

The first victim, Sophia Carew, was sixty-three, a brisk and active woman who had been living for some years as a paying guest in the home of a certain Colonel Baxeter and his wife. Herself of a military family, she had inherited an ample fortune and had spent many years in studying the Tuaregs, the Veiled People of the Sahara, about whom she had written a useful book called *Agades and the Veil*. She was no Gertrude Bell or even Freya Stark, but she had made a niche for herself, had been satisfied with her one book and had not tired everyone with unnecessary and artificially compounded sequels. She was tall, grey-haired, and stringy in appearance with a much-lined somewhat masculine face. She was a kind and friendly woman, beloved of her friends but with very few local acquaintances. She drove her own car and was rarely seen in the town.

She had come to Buddington, it seemed, because her only living relative resided there. Charlie Carew was her nephew, a man of forty whose cheerful thriftlessness and undergraduate alcoholism had been all very well when he was young but became rather tiresome now that he had got through most of his share of the family money and lived mysteriously, calling himself an insurance agent. He was a familiar figure in the saloon bars of the town, a good mixer, an inveterate hob-nobber, prone to narrative and the discussion of cricket scores. His wife had left him and he had few close friends, but was on mutual boring terms with most of the town.

On the Thursday of the murders Miss Carew had been up to town and reached Dehra Dun, Colonel Baxeter's house, at about six. She had joined her host and his wife in their customary cocktail and shared their evening meal at seven. She had gone out in her car afterwards, which was in no way unusual, for she was addicted both to the cinema and the local repertory theatre and shared the Colonel's detestation of television. It was not discovered until the morning that she had not slept in the house, for the Baxeters went to bed before ten and she had her latch-key. Mrs Baxeter went to her room with a cup of a beverage called Vita-Tea

—again according to custom—and found the bed unslept-in.

Even that did not unduly alarm the Baxeters, for Miss Carew was a strong-minded and independent woman who frequently did things on impulse. The Baxeters discussed the matter at breakfast and decided that the police should be informed, but without any panic. They expected a telephone call from Miss Carew all that morning, supposing that she had suddenly decided to return to town or something of the sort. She had never done such a thing before, they said, but they were not seriously perturbed.

Colonel Baxeter decided to call in person at the police station and report the matter, for he felt that Miss Carew might resent his raising an alarm over her movements. He wanted to explain the details and ask the police to use tact in their enquiries. However, before he left the house the Detective Inspector in charge called to give him the sad news that the body had been found.

There had, as a matter of fact, been very little attempt to conceal it. A disused quarry on the Lilbourne road, open to the highway, was scarcely a place to leave a corpse if it was hoped that no one would find it. Chance had brought it to light earlier than might be expected, but it could not in any case have remained long undiscovered. A roadmender working nearby was in the habit of leaving his tools concealed in the quarry overnight to avoid carrying them with him every day, and he had almost stumbled over the corpse of Sophia Carew.

Only two things were known generally about the condition of the corpse, but one of them added a macabre touch to the affair. Medical evidence was that Miss Carew had been strangled. She lay on her back, fully clothed and apparently laid out as though for burial. In her hands was clasped the stem of a somewhat crushed Madonna lily whose waxy white flowers lay on her breast.

Her car was found soon afterwards in the car-park of the Granodeon Cinema. No attendant remained there till the end of the last performance at half past ten, but the entrance to the car-park was locked by the cinema staff before they left the building, and since the padlock of the gate had not been interfered with it was presumed that the car could not have been put there later than that time.

In the car was her Kerry Blue terrier. He had apparently slept peacefully through the night, and there was nothing remarkable about this. Miss Carew frequently left him in the car while she was in the pictures, and while her car was in that place the poor creature had been quietly expecting her return.

So much for the first murder. The second differed from it in almost every circumstance except two, which were alarmingly similar.

Mrs Westmacott was not, like Miss Carew, a moderately well-to-do person; she was an extremely rich widow and made no bones about it. Her husband had died ten years previously; he was a son of Sefton Westmacott, a famous patron of the arts who had been a friend of the Rossettis and William Morris. Swinburne dedicated a poem to him and he figured in one of the paintings of Burne-Jones.

Sefton Westmacott junior, the husband of the murdered woman, had inherited his father's wealth, but had been a collector rather than an art-patron. Little was known of his wife's background, but she was rumoured to have been an artist's model. She was a stout and florid woman, considered in the town to be purse-proud but charitable, a staunch member of the congregation of St Augustine's, the 'high' church of Buddington. Indeed, although disliking to move about much she attended frequently at the church in a bathchair; otherwise she rarely left her home.

There were two sons and a daughter. Dante, the eldest of these, was married and owned a model farm five miles away, Gabriel, the younger son, lived with his mother, while Christina, the only daughter, had married a doctor in Middlesbrough and had not been in the town for a year.

Gabriel was the member of the family most determined to keep up the Pre-Raphaelite tradition. He had contributed several articles to magazines and gave lectures to provincial societies. He had confided in his mother that he had to deliver one of his lectures on The Pre-Raphaelites to a lecture society in Lancashire on what turned out to be the fatal Thursday night, and so would be absent from his home. A note had appeared in the local paper to this effect, though the name of the town in which he was to lecture had not been given. On the Wednesday afternoon he had caught a train to London.

Mrs Westmacott was therefore presumed to have been alone in the house on the fatal night. Her staff consisted of two women who came in daily and a married couple, who had been in her service for many years and lived in what had been the stables but were now converted into a comfortable dwelling for them.

There had been no forcible entry to Rossetti Lodge, so either her murderer had a key of the house or Mrs Westmacott herself had admitted him.

She had been found, also fully dressed, on a settee in her own sitting-room, also lying at full length on her back and holding a Madonna lily. She had been strangled and it was believed that she had died before midnight.

"What do you make of it?" asked the young waiter, whose name was Napper, when he realized that Carolus's interest had been caught.

"I don't want to make anything of it," said Carolus. "And if you'd ever had jaundice you'd know why."

Napper was inextinguishable.

"No, but it's rather fascinating, isn't it? The old girls had never met so far as anyone knows and there doesn't seem to be any connection between the families. So who could possibly have had a motive for killing both? Either, yes, but not both."

Carolus absently considered these last words. What

would the Fowlers say to them? Yet they were perfectly explicit.

"Whoever's due to come into Miss Carew's money could have done her, couldn't they? And the same with Mrs Westmacott's. But unless by some freak of chance there's a least common multiple—or would you say highest common factor?—I can't see who could have a motive. Yet those lilies suggest it was the same person."

"Unless . . ."

Napper put down the tray on to which he had collected the breakfast things and turned to Carolus.

"Unless what?" he asked.

"You spoke of a freak of chance. Suppose the murderer of Mrs Westmacott had seen the corpse of Miss Carew; couldn't he have adopted the same device to make it appear that both had been done by the same person?"

Napper grinned.

"Or if the murderer of Miss Carew knew how the corpse of Mrs Westmacott was to appear, couldn't he have done the same thing?"

"Or if two murderers had acted in concert, couldn't they have agreed to leave lilies to indicate that there was only one? Each would have an alibi to one murder, wouldn't he?"

"Or could it be a maniac, do you think, suddenly breaking out in Buddington? It would be the very place for him if he wants to specialize in strangling elderly women."

"Or why not suppose Miss Carew's murder was a try-out for the murder of Mrs Westmacott?"

"Or Mrs Westmacott's an encore for Miss Carew's?"

"You go too far," said Carolus.

"But you'll own it's intriguing, won't you? If it was one person he or she must have had a busy night. Miss Carew left her home before eight and Mrs Westmacott was dead before twelve. I suppose it's just possible, but it would have been rather a rush."

Carolus leaned back on the pillows.

"Don't talk to me about a rush," he said. "I'm resting."

"Do you want your lunch here?" asked Napper. "Or will you go down for it?"

He spoke as though they were old friends, yet his manner was not by modern standards impudent. He seemed a very self-confident and mature young man.

"I'll go down today, I think. I can't really pretend to be ill any more."

"Want to see the burial-chamber? We've a smashing collection of mummies."

He was about to open the door when Carolus asked: "Did you know either of the two murdered women, Napper?"

"Yes. Both," said the waiter. "They had both been here at different times. Mrs Westmacott only once."

"Recently?"

"Not for some weeks. Interested?"

"Not really," said Carolus.

He was not, he assured himself when he was alone.

It was a fine sunny morning and his room had a balcony facing south. He dressed and went out to it. The red-roofed town below him, the hills rolling away to the skyline, the springtime richness of the earth and the brilliant sky mottled with white clouds was reassuring. The scene had a fruitful look, as though England could live on her harvests. He had several weeks to pass idly and a number of books he had long wanted to read. Why should he be interested in the brutal murder of two elderly ladies? Why start again the old routine of enquiry, observation, deduction, analysis till a conclusion was reached and some wretched being was arrested, charged, tried and hanged?

Yet there were those disturbing questions. Two murderers or one? Conspiracy or independent action? It was impossible, having read the case, to avoid asking those.

There was a tap at the door and a pageboy brought in a

24

telegram which Carolus unwillingly opened and read: *Gorringer seething stop. What a bit of luck stop. Break-Up Tuesday shall I bring Bentley across or have you already solved. Stop. Free for holiday wire instructions. Priggley.*

"Any answer, sir?" asked the page.

"Yes. Wait a minute."

Carolus hurriedly scribbled: *Spend holiday with Hollingbournes stop. Nothing of interest here. Deene.*

He handed this to the boy but as he did so he was smiling.

3

WHEN Carolus came into the lounge of the hotel later that morning he gazed with some wonder on his fellow guests. He had no idea that survivals of this kind existed in such numbers. Old ladies with shawls and companions, old gentlemen with starched linen and monocles, they sat in deep armchairs from which nothing could rouse them but the time for lunch. Such younger people as there were in the room—and women of fifty looked positively girlish here —were obviously dependent relatives with or without expectations, or persons employed to ease the last years of wealthy old men and women. He himself, in his forties and weak and shaky from illness, felt a boy as he gazed about him.

He sat down, but was approached by a septuagenarian lady who had just entered.

"You'll excuse me," she said peremptorily, "but that's my seat."

Carolus rose.

"It has been for twelve years."

"I'm so sorry."

"You've evidently just arrived."

"Yes."

"They should have told you."

"Do you think I might venture on that armchair over there?"

"No. That's Lady Tonks's."

"I see. Perhaps . . ."

"You might sit there by the pillar, but Miss Stathey will be down in a minute. She'll want you to hear about her arthritis."

"Then where . . ."

"Keep clear of that party with the clergyman. Card-sharpers."

"Really?"

"I don't advise the Harbellows either. They were acquaintances of the late Mrs Westmacott. One doesn't want to be involved in anything like that."

"Certainly not."

"In a hotel like this where you may meet *anyone* you can't be too careful. Riff-raff. Nobodies. The hotel should refuse half of them. Tradespeople, in some cases."

"No!"

"I assure you of it."

"They look rather . . . retired sort of people."

"Retired from what? Of course if you want to associate with every Tom, Dick and Harry and very likely have your pocket picked, I don't want to discourage you. I knew this hotel before it Went Down."

"Yet you stay here . . ."

"Only while Sophia Carew was alive. Now that she has got herself murdered I shall leave. She mixed with the most extraordinary people. I told her a thousand times. Now you see the result."

"Quite. Did you know her well?"

"She was my cousin. Reckless, quite reckless. She would

talk to *anyone*. When you look round this hotel and see all the tag-rag and bobtail that come to such places nowadays you would think she could have been warned. But no. She was quite without discrimination. Look at the people she lived with. Baxeter, indeed."

"Isn't their name Baxeter?"

"I daresay their *name* is Baxeter, so far as it goes," said the old lady sharply. "But what does that signify?"

"I understand he's a retired Colonel?"

"Risen from the ranks, unless the army has gone down more than I thought. Oh, I believe perfectly worthy people in their own milieu. But fancy living with persons of that kind!"

The old lady was tall and thin and had a long sharp nose. The corners of her lips were pulled down to give her a hostile disapproving expression.

"Did you know Sophia Carew?" she asked Carolus, as though she had become suddenly aware of him standing beside her.

"No. I have just arrived in Buddington for a rest cure. My name is Deene. Spelt D-e-e-n-e."

"Is it? Spelt D-e-e-n-e. You may sit down. My name is Tissot."

But before Carolus could accept the invitation a pageboy came and told him that a gentleman was waiting to see him.

Miss Tissot heard this with a stony expression and when the boy added—"I believe he's a police inspector," the old lady set her lips and stared resolutely into the distance, scarcely acknowledging Carolus's leave-taking with a slight, an almost imperceptible, inclination of the head.

In the hall Carolus found his old friend Detective Inspector John Moore.

"I heard you'd arrived," said Moore. "Came round at once."

"But what are you doing here, John?"

27

"Been transferred. Just in time for this lot. Bright, isn't it?"

"Where can we get a drink? Do you think there's a bar in this place or will it only serve medicinal water?"

They found something called an American bar in which they were the only customers.

"Tell us all about it," said Carolus when they were sitting in a far corner.

"What? Oh, that," said Moore and was silent.

"Haven't they given you the case?"

"I've got the case all right."

"Teaser, is it?"

"In a way. Yet in a way open-and-shut. Look, Carolus. If I had to find the murderer of Sophia Carew I could do it. The nephew's as obvious a suspect as you could wish. Strongest possible motive, no alibi and a mass of other circumstantial stuff. If I was investigating the death of Mrs Westmacott I shouldn't have a doubt. The younger son . . ."

"But he was away in Lancashire, lecturing."

"Nothing of the sort. That was a blind. Told his mother that, he says, to get away from Buddington for a couple of nights. He again has a motive and no alibi. But how can I suspect Charlie Carew of killing Mrs Westmacott, or Gabriel Westmacott of killing Miss Carew?"

"I see your difficulty. No suspect fits both?"

"None. Yet there's every indication that it was the same person."

"Madonna lilies, you mean?"

"And other small points. However, you've come here for a rest, I understand."

"I shouldn't mind hearing what you know."

"That's not the hell of a lot. But for what it's worth you can have it. First of all, the wills."

"How you do go straight to money, don't you, John?"

"I've rarely known it to fail, unless it's a crime of passion,

28

which you could scarcely call this. Sophia Carew's will was a very simple and straightforward document. There were no small legacies. All she had was to be divided into three equal parts. One went to the nephew, Charles Carew, one to the couple in whose house she lived, Garnett and Mor Baxeter, and the third to a cousin Martha Tissot."

"Martha, eh?"

"Anything wrong?"

"Nothing. But I know the lady. Go on."

"Mrs Westmacott's was a much more complicated affair and she had more to leave. There were legacies to the Bickleys, the man and wife who had worked for her for years, to various literary and artistic societies, to local charities connected with St Augustine's church and to someone named Grace Lightfoot. There was also a sizeable legacy to a former lady's maid of hers married to a man called Thickett. The rest goes to her children, but not in equal proportions. The eldest son, Dante, gets as much as the other two, Gabriel and Christina, put together."

"Nice range of suspects if you're right in thinking money's the motive."

"Now as to the bodies. Medical examination has revealed no sign of a struggle in either case. Both women had been strangled with something soft like a scarf which left no abrasions. Mrs Westmacott is believed to have died somewhere round about midnight and Miss Carew about two hours earlier. Each had been laid flat on her back with the lily stem in her clasped hands."

"Have you kept the stems?"

"Of course."

"How many flowers to each?"

"Are you being funny?"

"No. I've a reason for asking."

"Three each, I believe."

"Had there been more?"

"I daresay. Why?"

"But you didn't notice? Listen, John, phone to your office and ask, will you?"

"I thought you were resting."

Moore was absent a few minutes and came back to say that one had originally had five blooms, the other four. Carolus thanked him quite seriously.

"Miss Carew's body," continued Moore, "was found by a roadmender called Thickett. He swears that except when he took hold of the arm to shake Miss Carew who, he thought, was asleep, he did not touch the body. He cycled down to the call-box at the cross roads and phoned us. I was in the office and went out myself."

"Good."

"It was, our records tell us, an extremely dark and cloudy night, but there was no rain. The ground was fairly soft and we were able to distinguish some footprints, of which we have casts."

"Really. Footprints, eh? It's years since I remember footprints being used as evidence."

"I don't know that they will be. You see, they were size eight (men's), and as you know this can mean almost anything. From what I can gather of this murderer he wouldn't just have overlooked the question of footprints. A man, however large his feet (unless they were truly abnormal), could squeeze into a pair of shoes size eight if the laces had been removed. Or, however small his feet were, he could walk in them for a short distance. Also, most women could do the same."

"What makes you suppose anyone did? Your murderer, knowing his shoes were of a popular size, might have just kept his own on. Why should you think he didn't?"

"Because an old pair of shoes, men's, size eight, was found in the ditch between the road and the quarry. They had been worn by whoever left the footprints."

"Had they, by jove? This *is* getting interesting. Have they been identified?"

30

"No, but they had been newly soled and heeled by a shoemaker called Humpling. He says that six months or more ago a pair of shoes was missing from his shop. He cannot swear these are the ones, but he is sure these were repaired by him. Of the people so far connected with the case he appears to know Mrs Westmacott's servants the Bickleys and a man called Wright, who is chauffeur to your friend Miss Tissot. We are trying to trace the owner of the shoes that were missing from Humpling's shop."

"Back to the quarry, John. What else was found?"

"Evidence that the body had been dragged from the car to where it was lying. The clothes would have told us this in any case, but the research boys have been over the ground and say there's no doubt of it."

"Any trace of the car itself?"

"None. It must have stood clear of the verge."

"No one see it?"

"We've had no report of anything of the kind. We've had no help at all. Even the medical evidence is vague. Our man is very chary of giving the exact time of death. He says, and I daresay he's right, that nine times out of ten that's a lot of nonsense and no doctor can tell to an hour, let alone less. It depends on a thousand factors—temperature of the air, state of the murdered person and so on. Beyond saying that he thought Miss Carew had been dead longer than Mrs Westmacott he wouldn't for a long time commit himself. But in the end he agreed that Miss Carew was probably killed in the early part of the evening, before ten he conjectures, and Mrs Westmacott towards midnight. But he will not give evidence of that on oath, he says. It's just his feeling on the subject."

"Fair enough. I'd rather have that than one of those doctors who look at a cadaver for a moment then say it has been dead for precisely eighteen and a half hours. Wouldn't you?"

"Yes. It's more honest. But his information doesn't help

us much. He is quite convinced, however, that both the women were strangled with something soft like a silk scarf, probably drawn tight from behind."

"It's the most usual method, isn't it? What information have you about the murder of Mrs Westmacott?"

"There's even less to tell you. She was a large woman, older than Sophia Carew but upstanding still. Rather imposing, in a way. She was found in a little sitting-room she used in the evening and there must have been a big fire in the grate till quite late that night, because the embers were still hot in the morning."

"Who found her?"

"Mrs Bickley. She came across as usual at eight o'clock and found the corpse before she had been up to the bedroom. She describes Mrs Westmacott as looking 'horror-struck'. She cannot understand why she was not summoned on the previous evening, since there is a telephone communicating with the Bickleys' rooms across the yard."

"Any signs of a struggle?"

"None. It would seem that the woman was already sitting on the settee on which her body was found. The murderer probably gave some excuse for passing round the back of it and neatly strangled her before she could raise any alarm."

"No fingerprints, of course?"

"None, needless to say, of anybody except the household. The days when murderers obligingly signed their masterpieces are over, Carolus. There was, however, one rather curious thing found in the room which neither the Bickleys nor any member of the Westmacott family admits seeing before. It looks like something off a Christmas tree. It's a thin wire with a number of those sparkling things you have for the kids at Christmas. The wire is about a foot long and has been wound round these things at about two inch intervals."

"There are six of them then?"

"Seven, actually. But it hadn't been used to strangle the

old woman or anything like that. The sparklets or whatever you call them were quite intact. Besides she, like Sophia Carew, had been strangled with something soft."

"Where was it found?"

"On a little table behind the settee."

"Anything else?"

"No. I don't think so."

"What about Sophia Carew's car?"

"It was in the car-park of the Granodeon Cinema. The attendant there went off duty at nine and is almost sure it wasn't there when he left. There were no fingerprints to speak of on the car, but then people naturally have worn gloves during recent weather. Charlie Carew admits to having driven with his aunt several times lately, though; also the Baxeters and once Martha Tissot, though she has got her own car, as I told you. That's about the lot, Carolus. See any wood for trees?"

"Not really, I'm afraid."

"We're rather inclined to think it's a maniac. In that case there's always anxiety about another possible murder. Heaven knows there are plenty of elderly women in this town, and one's apt to wonder which will be found holding lilies."

"Is there *nothing* to connect the two murders?"

"You can imagine that we've tried pretty hard to find something. Certain tradesmen serve the two, but I don't think they had any mutual acquaintances. There is one thing which I'll tell you, for what it's worth. They had both sold some gold recently to a gold-clapper called Maurice Ebony."

"What's a gold-clapper?"

"You're not much up in anything but murder, are you, Carolus? You should have more all-round experience. A gold-clapper is a man who runs round on the knock buying gold from private houses. He has a good many tricks and fiddles, but there's not much we can do about it. A week or so before these murders Ebony, who is a London man and in quite a big way, was working this district. He has a woman runner who makes his appointments for him, a very attractive girl called Moira Long. She got in to see the Baxeters and Ebony bought some stuff from them. While he was doing so Sophia Carew came in and was persuaded to sell him some old-fashioned jewellery. On the following day Moira Long called at Rossetti Lodge and Ebony had what he describes as a gobble. It's probably entirely irrelevant, but it's the only small link we can find between the two households."

"He must have bought a lot more in Buddington, though?"

"Not so much as you'd think. This place is a natural for gold-clappers and has been worked over again and again. Now, Carolus, you can get the old brain working and if you have any of your improbable ideas you might let me know. We shall go on in our plodding way, of course."

"All right, John. Come and see me again, won't you?"

4

For the next three days Carolus found himself, in common with the other guests at the Royal Hydro, severely cut by Miss Tissot. Before lunch he would approach her but found that she was immersed in a novel by Charles Morgan and did not look up as he passed. When tea was served in the lounge she appeared to concentrate on her cup if Carolus was near, and although before dinner she made her appearance in a dress such as a Court governess might wear if she was to be present at a state dinner-party, she refused to let Carolus catch her eye.

He had so much recovered during those three days, however, that on the fourth he decided mischievously to put a stop to Miss Tissot's frigid unawareness of him. Taking his newspaper he reached the lounge earlier than usual and settled himself in Miss Tissot's chair. Then he opened his paper and appeared to be lost in it. He felt rather than saw the old lady's approach, but when she spoke it was without any hesitation or ambiguity.

"You have taken my seat again. The first time it may have been a stupid blunder—this is insolence."

Carolus rose at once with a smile.

"No, intrigue," he said. "I wanted to talk to you."

Miss Tissot made no reply as she sat down and opened *Sparkenbroke*.

"What a *bore* Charles Morgan was," said Carolus rudely. "Or don't you think?"

"One can tell by his books that he was a gentleman," said the old lady, fiercely and truthfully.

"Miss Tissot, do you want to know who murdered your cousin?"

"I want to know as little as possible about it. It is bad enough that my cousin should have been found dead in a ditch. It is worse that her death should be associated with that of a woman known to be a vulgar and bohemian sort of person. An artist's model, I believe."

"You don't think they were victims of the same assailant, then?"

"I have no opinion on the subject. My cousin had so little discrimination that anything is possible. I attended the inquest much against my will. As soon as Miss Carew's affairs are settled I shall leave Buddington and never return."

"Wouldn't it be more satisfactory to have the matter cleared up?"

"What, exactly, are you proposing, Mr Deene?"

"I want your authority to investigate."

"Surely the police will do that?"

"Of course. But I believe I could get at the truth of the matter with some discretion. I need the authority of someone closely concerned. I do not want to approach the Westmacott family for that."

"Do you think you can save me from further unwelcome publicity?"

"I would try."

"You are, I understand, some kind of private detective?"

"Some kind, yes. Rather a peculiar kind. I never concern myself with anything but murder."

"It sounds a morbid pursuit. Do I understand that you are asking for a fee?"

"None. I shall do it because it interests me."

"You seem a fairly respectable young man, in spite of your impertinence in twice appropriating my chair. And your name is spelt D-e-e-n-e. I will consider the matter."

"Thank you, Miss Tissot. Now can I persuade you to drink an aperitif with me?"

"Sherry and bitters," said Miss Tissot before Carolus had finished speaking. She spoke decisively.

"Excellent," said Carolus and called the waiter. "Who do you think killed your cousin?"

"I find speculation on the subject most distasteful and quite fruitless. It cannot have been anyone sane, surely?"

"Sanity can cover a multitude of aberrations, though. It might be someone who is accepted by the world as sane, I think. I shall hope to tell you a little more about that if you give me your authority to make a few enquiries."

"I will give you that."

"The first I wish to make relates to your chauffeur, Harold Wright."

"Indeed? And what has Wright to do with it?"

"He knew Miss Carew?"

"He had driven her, on occasion."

"He has been with you some years?"

"Since he was five years old. He is the son—I regret to say the *natural* son—of an excellent cook I had when I kept up our home at Ventnor. His mother died when he was seventeen and he has remained in my service."

"He's a good chauffeur?"

"He is most devoted. Unfortunately, my lawyers have recently informed me that I am not justified in the expense of maintaining a motor-car. It seems some investments made by my father have not appreciated as they should. As I now live entirely in hotels the car is a most expensive luxury."

"Wright knew this?"

"I had felt it best to give him a preliminary warning. He was most distressed. Since I have learned the terms of my cousin's will I realize that I shall be able to keep the car. But I really cannot see what connection this has with . . ."

"Oh, none. Miss Carew seems to have had a very small acquaintance and Wright was known to her."

"Small acquaintance? My cousin was far too indiscriminate. It does not do to hob-nob with every kind of canaille. She would probably be alive now if she had listened to my advice in this matter. No one can be too careful in a place like this."

"Have you any particular reason for saying this, Miss Tissot? Was there someone of whom you particularly disapproved?"

"No. But her whole manner of life showed lack of discernment. She lived with these so-called Baxeters . . ."

"Did you know them?"

"Know them? Certainly not. I shouldn't dream of being acquainted with such people. They had made their home a common lodging-house."

"But Miss Carew was their only paying guest, I understand?"

"Numbers, Mr Deene, are irrelevant. They let rooms. I can only suppose that my unfortunate cousin inherited the

37

prodigality with which she made friends from her father. Her mother, you see, was my father's sister and married a man called Carew, a clergyman whose very profession brought him into contact with the most undesirable people. This is even more apparent in her disreputable nephew, Charles."

"Is he disreputable?"

"Utterly. But what can you expect?"

"Nothing. I know very little about him."

"His father was an artist."

"That surely . . ."

"Not even an Academician. Fortunately, he had money of his own."

"There seem to be a number of artists connected with this case."

"I have told you, my cousin was quite without discrimination. I can well believe her death has associations of that sort."

"Did Charles Carew inherit his father's talent?"

"I do not know that his father had any talent. And talent, Mr Deene, is only too apt to make people forget their place."

"I see what you mean."

"As for Charles Carew I had nothing to do with him. He was not a blood relation of mine. His father was Sophia's father's brother. I gather he did everything possible to distress Sophia's father, who at least was a clergyman."

"What sort of thing?"

"He was an artist of the old and most disreputable school. A Bohemian, a vagabond, a character from the Latin Quarter who looked the part."

"That certainly sounds rather shocking."

"For a time he even lived in Paris, I believe."

An exodus had started from the lounge. Walking sticks were seized with alacrity to assist the guests, making their way to the dining-room, their faces brightened by the prospect of lunch. Old ladies leaned on the arms of younger

38

ones, but managed to move at a surprising pace; elderly gentlemen ignoring all about them resolutely threaded their way between the tables. Only a few stragglers paused to leave books or needlework on their chairs to reserve them.

In the huge dining-room there was no time wasted with conversation. The waiters rushed forward, like hospital nurses in an emergency case, to hand out menus, which were studied with ferocious concentration through every variety of seeing-aid, from normal spectacles to old-fashioned pince-nez and lorgnettes.

"I haven't got my glasses," wailed an old lady at a table near Carolus. "Read it to me, Annie dear. Read it to me." It was a cry from the heart.

Across the room, alone at a table like himself, Martha Tissot was as busy as the rest.

Napper appeared beside him.

"Sorry to keep you waiting," he said in a man-to-man way; "I had to get 'em going first. Hell breaks loose if they're kept waiting. Tell you what's good if you're hungry. Boiled silverside and dumplings. *Boeuf bouilli aux boudinettes* this bloody fool of a cook calls it, though why I can't think. He's from Chiswick and his name's Wilkes. Beer? Yes. I'll bring you in a pint. It'll shake 'em in here. They toy with a sip of white wine usually."

Finding his appetite returning with his energy, Carolus felt better than he had for weeks. He realized that he had committed himself now to entanglement in the murder case in the town, but decided to take it easily. He found the problem an intriguing one, but since John Moore was in charge he could think of it without urgency and without any sense of responsibility. John would unravel it, all right; he, Carolus, could regard it as a chance to exercise his hobby.

As he left the dining-room he was called to the telephone. A Mr Gabriel Westmacott wanted to speak to him.

"Mr Deene?" came a fruity voice. "My name's Gabriel

39

Westmacott. I have read a book of yours and I wanted to see you."

"How did you know I was here?" asked Carolus, rather sharply.

"Oh it gets around, you know. May I come and see you?"

"Perhaps you would say what you want to see me about?"

Carolus expected an evasive answer, but no, it came pat.

"My mother's murder," said Gabriel Westmacott.

Carolus considered quickly, then said: "Would you please call here about four today?"

"I will, with pleasure."

At four o'clock the room designated 'Residents' Writing-Room' was empty, since the guests were mustering in the great Palm Lounge for afternoon tea. Carolus had given instructions in the lobby and went there to await his man.

Gabriel Westmacott was tall and pale, his long auburn hair was silvering a little and he had innocent-looking pale blue eyes. Even in his appearance there was something unmistakably Pre-Raphaelite, and his movements, his white skin and look of a middle-aged angel confirmed it. He smoked with a cigarette-holder.

"When I heard you were in the town I could not help guessing the object of your stay," he said. There was something supercilious in his manner which Carolus found hard to bear. "My mother's death must have been irresistible to you."

"I was here before it happened," said Carolus shortly. "I came to recuperate after an illness."

"In that case it must be very fortunate for you. You have a diverting problem laid on your doorstep, as it were."

"What did you want to see me about?"

"Just that. I cannot believe that you're not going to take up the case."

"So?"

40

"I should like you to act on my behalf."

"I'm afraid that's impossible. I am already committed."

"My brother Dante?"

"No. I'm acting for the cousin of Miss Carew."

"I never knew she had a cousin."

"You were acquainted with Miss Carew?"

"No. That is, I had seen her. I had read her book."

"When did you see her last?"

"Oh come now, Mr Deene. Don't begin to question me, please. I have had enough of that from the police. I came to enlist your aid."

"Have you any suspicions at all about your mother's death?"

"None. I know of no enemies. The only people who benefit from it are her legatees, and I don't suppose the most suspicious person would think that I or my brother would strangle my mother for her money."

"There were other legatees."

"Yes, but . . . I really think that is a fruitless line of enquiry."

"What do you think then, Mr Westmacott?"

"Someone with a penchant for murdering old ladies, surely? The lilies argue that, I feel."

"Yet you say the police have questioned you?"

"Rigorously, yes. And that is the unfortunate thing. You see, I was in the town that evening and the police are aware of it."

"Awkward, that. You were supposed to be lecturing in Lancashire."

"I do quite often lecture and it nearly always seems to be Lancashire or Yorkshire or some place to which the fare costs almost as much as the lecture fee. But this time I wanted, frankly, a couple of nights in London. I left on the Wednesday morning, stayed Wednesday night . . ."

"Where?"

"I beg your pardon?"

"Where did you stay?"

"That surely has nothing to do with it. It was on Thursday night that my mother and Miss Carew were murdered."

"A hotel?"

"No. A private flat, as a matter of fact. Friends."

"I see," said Carolus pointedly.

"On Thursday I felt I couldn't come tamely back here for another long period on the following day. But I had run out of money and also I thought I should tell my mother what I was doing. So I drove down here."

"What is the exact distance from London?"

"Thirty-seven miles."

"You left London at?"

"Eight o'clock. Reached my mother's house a little before ten. She was alone in the little sitting-room in which she was found next day."

"Oh, you saw her?"

"Certainly. I was with her for about an hour. I explained that I wanted a few days' holiday. She gave me the money I required."

"A cheque?"

"No. My mother kept a large sum in cash in the house. She gave me sixty pounds."

"Where did she keep that money?"

"In her bedroom, somewhere. I don't know exactly. She went upstairs to fetch it."

"Has the remains of her hoard been found since, do you know?"

"I don't know. I parted with my mother at eleven. She was in excellent health and spirits. I drove away and reached London soon after midnight."

"Have you any proof of that? It would make an excellent alibi for you, if you have."

"I haven't, I'm afraid. I had a latch-key of the flat where I was staying and nobody was up. But I think it's rather absurd to talk about alibis. Surely no one in their senses could suspect me of murdering my mother?"

"My dear Mr Westmacott, in these days of schizophrenia anyone may be suspected of anything. Somebody entered your mother's house that evening, either with his own key or by her consent. It limits the field quite a little, doesn't it?"

The long pale face remained expressionless.

"You think the police may even be foolish enough to suspect me?"

"You must be on the list of possibles for anyone investigating these murders. I take it you don't wish to give details of your movements in London?"

"No. They had absolutely nothing to do with this."

"Tell me a little about your mother, Mr Westmacott."

"My mother was nearing eighty years old. You have probably seen photographs of her. She was considered a very handsome woman. She had a wide acquaintance among artists and writers, particularly those who were interested in the Pre-Raphaelite school. She inherited my father's collection of William Morris textiles, pottery, books and furniture, and although she was not precisely what you would call an intellectual woman she appreciated these and was proud of our family connection with that famous circle of craftsmen. She liked to invite people who were interested to the house, and entertained very freely."

"You were all brought up in this atmosphere, then. Weren't you apt to rebel at times? I should have thought you had had enough of Burne-Jones and whatnot."

Gabriel Westmacott blinked solemnly.

"I believe my brother Dante is less interested than I. His wife is not of an art-loving disposition, by any means. For my own part I am proud to be the grandson of a man who was familiar with those giants."

"Was your mother's kindness to artists appreciated?"

"Almost universally. There were exceptions, of course.

43

Or at least one exception. A disreputable painter called Ben Johnson. . . ."

"But he's considered one of our most remarkable living artists."

Gabriel Westmacott seemed to have something uncomfortably hot in his mouth.

"I know nothing about his pictures. He is a dissolute man, given to drunkenness and other vices. His language is abominable and he is unable to control his violent temper and outrageous manners in the presence of ladies."

"You know him?"

"I know of him. He lives not far away and is notorious as a rake and a rowdy. When he first came here my mother was good enough to invite him to the house, but he declined in the most offensive terms."

"So your mother never met him?"

"No. Never. She was so unwisely generous as to repeat her invitation, which was made by letter on a later occasion, possibly more than once. I think she felt that it was a pity that a painter, however undisciplined his private life, should be living and working near Rossetti Lodge and remain unknown to her. But he either ignored her invitation or replied in ribald terms."

"He's a fine painter," said Carolus.

"That," said Gabriel Westmacott, "is a matter of opinion. I venture to doubt, however, whether any of the great men whose names I revere, the associates of my grandfather, would have been able to bear the sight of his mangled atrocities."

"Quite," said Carolus adequately. "I shall probably want to ask you some more later, Mr Westmacott, when I have gone farther into this thing."

"I shall be prepared to answer," said Gabriel solemnly, "but I should like to know now whether you have formed any suspicion."

"None, except that I do not believe the two murders were

44

the work of a maniac with a lust for killing. I believe that there was calculated motive behind them."

"Indeed!" said Gabriel Westmacott and soon after took his leave.

5

ON the following Tuesday Rupert Priggley walked into Carolus's room before he was up.

"I thought I told you to spend your Easter holidays with the Hollingbournes?" said Carolus snappily.

"I thought that was your rather immature idea of humour, sir," said Carolus's least favourite pupil. "They're going to Cornwall. I couldn't have stood saffron cake and art colonies, even if the Hollingbournes themselves were not unthinkable. There are four children, you know, three male and a girl of seven. But let's come to realities. You've taken on the case, of course?"

"I suppose so. In a rather half-hearted way. I haven't started investigating."

"Good. Then the Bentley will be useful."

Carolus sat up in bed.

"You haven't had the impertinence to drive my car without permission?"

"Calm now, sir. Calm before all. It's outside, in perfect condition. I missed both an insane lorry-driver and a woman in a Wolseley."

"You insolent young blackguard . . ."

"No, no, sir. It's my biological equipment that's at fault. My responses are out of harmony with the social forces. Nothing organic, no endocrine disorder or anything like

45

that. It's due to an over-aggressive and defiant behaviour pattern during the growth process. I'm an over-compensated psychopath . . ."

"You're a rat. Give me the car keys. I suppose you'll have to lunch with me before I send you back. Go down and wait in the lounge."

Rupert grinned.

"I thought you'd succumb," he said. "Who do we interview first?"

Carolus went alone that afternoon to Dehra Dun, the home of Colonel and Mrs Baxeter. The name had led Carolus to imagine a house full of Benares ware and trophies with tiger skins on the floor and the triumphs of taxidermy grinning down from every wall. Not a bit of it. Dehra Dun had been named by a previous occupant and the house was notable for its windows of some health-giving glass, its violet ray lamps, its open baskets of fruit and vegetables arranged as ornaments. It had the carpetless appearance of an expensive hospital.

Colonel Baxeter was a little brown wrinkled man with strong white hair, bright blue eyes and an excessively washed and hygienic appearance. His wife was a Brunnhilde.

"We're nudists," said the Colonel alarmingly, as though to explain the open windows and his own open shirt on this chilly day.

"And vegetarians," added his wife.

"Really? And did Miss Carew share your views?"

"Not altogether. She had our detestation of stuffy, unhealthy rooms," said the Colonel, ignoring Carolus's shiver. "But she was not a member of the Vegetarian Society."

"Nor of the Naturist League," put in Mrs Baxeter whose habit it was to add a footnote to her husband's remarks.

"She took a certain amount of alcohol," went on the Colonel. "To our own cocktail, a delicious mixture of natural fruit juices, she added a modicum of gin. She had

46

not our abhorrence for meat on the ground that it is full of excretory substances and is tissue-destroying in man."

"Also that flesh-eating involves an immense volume of pain for sentient animals."

"Quite," said the Colonel. "We did not, of course, impose our views on our guest and her own diet was prepared for her. She also smoked, though my wife and I would not think of damaging our lungs with tobacco smoke."

"Or sacrificing our good health to the vice of nicotine."

"No? But she was a very healthy woman, I believe?"

"She was no more unhealthy than others who have these habits. You are investigating her death, I think?"

"I'm trying to find out who killed her. I should like to ask you a few questions, if I may."

"By all means," said the Colonel. "We are anxious to render every assistance. In many respects we had a strong regard and affection for Sophia."

"You have no idea where she intended to go when she left you that evening?"

"None. It was not her habit to apprise us of her movements. She frequently went to the cinema, for instance, but knowing that the very thought of its smoky and unhealthy atmosphere was painful to us, she rarely mentioned it. That evening she said at dinner that she was going out. That was all."

"There was the phone call," remembered his wife.

"Ah yes. While we were having our evening fruit cocktail the phone rang and I answered it. The call came from a phone box. I distinctly heard the pennies drop. A high-pitched voice asked for Miss Carew."

"Do you mean a woman's voice?"

"Not necessarily. It was an artificial and squeaky voice which might have been assumed by a man disguising his own. Sophia went to the phone, which is in the hall, and we did not hear her conversation. But we did hear her a few minutes later shouting into the phone as though she was trying to make a deaf person hear. 'Can't you *hear* me?' she said several times, then, as though exasperated, put the receiver down. It was shortly after this that she said she was going out."

"Did she seem at all worried?"

"No. Elated if anything. She mentioned that she would take Skylark with her. This referred to her dog, a Kerry Blue. She was extremely fond of animals of all kinds, a taste which we could not share. Sophia was a member of the Royal Zoological Society and frequently spent days at the Zoo. This was unaccountable to us, who cannot bear to see any animal in captivity."

"Even a dog?" asked Carolus.

"There you touch another matter. My wife and I object to domestic animals not on ethical grounds but because we find it unhygienic to share living quarters with germ-carriers and carnivores."

"But you allowed Miss Carew to keep Skylark?"

"There is a yard in which the dog could enjoy a certain liberty and at the same time be isolated from our living-rooms. But Sophia had him to sleep in her room, took him for walks, even fondled him. He invariably occupied the seat beside her in her motor-car, so that when my wife and I drove with her we sat at the back. Even had we wished to sit otherwise I do not think the dog could have been induced to yield his seat, a state of things which I find open to criticism."

"But Skylark was a well-behaved dog," said Mrs Baxeter.

"Where is he now?" asked Carolus.

"In this back yard behind the house. He was found in Sophia's car in the car-park of the cinema on the morning after the murder."

"Miss Carew had many friends?"

"In Buddington very few. She was a member of a London club and had a wide acquaintance in town. But not here."

"Who, for instance?"

48

"Her cousin, Miss Tissot, for whom you are acting. We have not met her, though it is our hope and intention very shortly to meet her. We are co-beneficiaries under Sophia's will and I feel that we should become acquainted. Then there was Sophia's nephew, Charles. We do not care for him, but out of our regard for Sophia we have entertained him here on several occasions."

"What's wrong with him?"

"Nothing, I daresay, if you view life as he does. We found him altogether lacking in idealism."

"Materialistic," added Mrs Baxeter.

"Of recent years he has deteriorated badly. He was a healthier man when his wife was with him. They were enthusiastic cyclists."

"Really? That seems very out of character."

"It is with the Charles Carew of today. He has become a gross eater. If not a sot, at least a heavy consumer of alcohol. But we have rather high standards for our friends. I do not condemn the man. I say merely that he was not quite the type we should normally have encouraged."

"Anyone else?"

"Sophia was acquainted with a man named Ben Johnson, a painter I believe."

This was said in a peculiarly stony manner. It was evident that the Baxeters disapproved far more strongly of the painter than of Charlie Carew.

"He is a very good painter," said Carolus.

"I should prefer not to discuss him. On the only occasion on which we met his language in front of my wife, indeed his whole presence, was most offensive."

"Intolerable," said Mrs Baxeter.

"Had Miss Carew any visitors lately?"

"Yes. About a week ago Gabriel Westmacott called."

Carolus showed his surprise.

"I understood that Miss Carew and the Westmacotts were unacquainted."

"They were. She had never met Gabriel Westmacott. He called one afternoon and we were present when she received him. In this room, as a matter of fact. It seemed he had come to ask her a favour."

"How very odd. What was it?"

"It appeared that his mother, who does not leave her house very much, is apt to consider her drawing-room as something of a salon. She had through her husband some affiliation with the Pre-Raphaelites and William Morris. For years now, we gathered, she has sought to include this Mr Johnson in her circle. I find it inexplicable, of course, but Mrs Westmacott was a rich woman and accustomed to fulfilling her whims. She was aware that Sophia was friendly with Johnson and all else having failed she had sent her son to make a personal representation to Sophia to assist her. I think Sophia was amused. She shared our distaste for that kind of snobbery and tuft-hunting."

"What you tell me is most interesting, Colonel Baxeter. It constitutes almost the only known link between the two cases. Any other visitors?"

"There was a person buying old gold," said Colonel Baxeter. "We recommended him to her notice. His assistant called here one morning, a pleasant young woman who gave her name as Moira Long, and when my wife said she might find some pieces of old jewellery she no longer wanted she made an appointment for her principal to call that afternoon. He was a most presentable and reasonable person, who purchased what gold we had at the fixed rate. We were perfectly satisfied and recommended him to Sophia. She too sold him certain articles, but a heavy gold chain which she had always supposed to be gold turned out to be silver gilt."

"How did you know that?"

"Mr Ebony, the buyer, scraped the surface with a small file and showed her the silver under the plating."

"The whitewash," said Carolus.

"I beg your pardon?"

"Nothing. Just an old gold-buyer's trick. When he had filed the surface he rubbed his thumb over it to clear the filings away. But his thumb had just touched the silver nitrate paste under the lapel of his jacket and made the rough surface appear silver."

"If that's the case he succeeded in defrauding Sophia."

"I'm sorry."

"You seem to have an intimate knowledge of the subject," said the Colonel severely.

Carolus smiled.

"It happens that I have just looked it up. I was, in fact, caught unawares when it was mentioned to me. A kind of fraud of which I had no knowledge at all. Now, was there anyone else?"

"I don't think so. I can't remember anyone."

"The chauffeur," said Mrs Baxeter.

"Oh yes. Miss Tissot's chauffeur Wright came a week or two back when Sophia's car was out of order. Her cousin had sent him to drive Sophia somewhere. I forget where. He wasn't very pleased when she insisted on taking Skylark in the car, I remember."

Carolus's interrogation and the Colonel's willing answers were interrupted by Mrs Baxeter, who invited them to have some tea.

"Thank you," said Carolus and ventured to add, "I suppose we couldn't have the windows closed for a little while, could we? I'm recovering from jaundice and not quite as Spartan as you in the matter of fresh air."

With a suggestion of reluctance the Colonel closed the windows and after the icy air of the last hour the room seemed comparatively warm. Mrs Baxeter produced tea and to Carolus's relief it appeared to be the normal brew.

"We sometimes drink *maté*, a splendid beverage from South America," said the Colonel, "and sometimes an excellent preparation called Vita-Tea. But we have no objection to tea; we are less severe than many vegetarians and indulge in both milk and butter, though animal products. Have a piece of this fruitarian date cake? No? A nut finger? Oatcake? Wholemeal bread and groundnut butter? You remind me of poor Sophia. She never ate at teatime. It is one of our favourite meals. You should have a sandwich—Mock Salmon paste. That's homemade jam, carrot and marigold. Can't tempt you?"

"A biscuit, Mr Deene? Those are charcoal and hazelnut. Or another cup of tea?"

"Thank you," said Carolus. "There's one thing I want to clear up. It is said that Miss Carew was totally unacquainted with the Westmacott family and that there was no connecting link at all. Except for that call by Gabriel Westmacott, was that the case?"

"Not quite. For some years it has been our habit to drive from time to time to Dante Westmacott's farm near Lilbourne, where we purchase fresh produce, uncontaminated by handling in the market. Mr Westmacott has come here on occasion and once met Sophia at lunch."

"I see. There was no particular friendship between them?"

"Oh, none. I am certain that was the only time they met."

"You never knew Mrs Westmacott senior?"

"No."

"You did not for instance attend St Augustine's church?"

"We are Pantheists," said the Colonel severely. "We do not believe in individual substantial souls but in one universal vital sensitive force permeating the world like an all-pervading breath. The hotch-potch of obscurantism and superstition which would be found in the place you mention would be poisonous to us. Our cathedral is the open air."

"Very pleasant," said Carolus absently. "And Miss Carew?"

52

"Her attitude was a negative one. She certainly attended no church."

"If she had met Mrs Westmacott you would have known?"

"Undoubtedly. She was most communicative about anyone in the town she knew. When Gabriel came here she told us that she had never seen him before and knew none of his family."

"Did anything come of his visit and the request he made?"

"Nothing. Only on that last night at dinner she said lightly that she would have to mention it to the man Johnson, to whom she referred as 'Ben', unaware that such familiarity pained us."

"One other point, Colonel Baxeter. Miss Carew's will. You know the terms of it?"

"Yes. Her solicitor has communicated with me. It came as a surprise. We were very old friends; in fact it might be said that we were brought up together. My father was a doctor in Colchester when her father held a living in the neighbourhood. It was very gratifying to us both when Sophia came to share our home and I think I may say that she was happy with us. But that she should leave us so large a portion of her estate has astounded us. Naturally, we could wish that it had not come to us through such a tragic event and we are as shocked as anyone at the manner of her death. Nonetheless it would be hypocritical not to admit that the money will be useful."

"It always is," said Carolus and was silent.

"Have no hesitation if there is anything else you wish to ask."

"Nothing factual, Colonel Baxeter. But surely you who knew Miss Carew so well must have some suspicion?"

For the first time the Colonel seemed at a loss. Presently he answered in his usual unruffled manner.

"My wife and I do not allow ourselves to indulge in

suspicion at the expense of other human beings," he said. "Our creed is of brotherhood."

"Yes, yes, but somebody deliberately strangled your friend."

"I cannot allow myself to suppose that it was deliberate, Mr Deene, at least in the sense you use the word. No one sane, no one of healthy mind, could have done such a thing."

"I see what you mean. Those lilies."

"We disapprove of cutting flowers. We do not allow the air in our home to be polluted by the fumes that rise from decaying vegetation. It seems to me that the placing of those flowers on the dead body was consistent with the act of murder itself."

"Really?"

"Yes. Quite consistent. It is the murder which seems to us the work of a mind unhinged. Once that is recognized the details follow. You surely agree that the murders were committed by a homicidal maniac?"

"No, I do not. And I don't think the police accept that idea."

"You surprise me."

Carolus rose to go.

"Sophia had no troubles that we knew of, no anxieties. No problems," volunteered the Colonel.

"That makes it very baffling. Thank you so much for all your information."

Colonel Baxeter came with him to the door and Carolus hurried out to his car and drove straight to the Royal Hydro. He felt chilled to the bone. The hygienic air of Dehra Dun had, he thought, brought him near to a relapse. He ruthlessly pushed his way to a seat near one of the great log fires in the lounge and after removing a magazine and bag left to reserve it sank into its cosy depths. He then lit a cigarette, drew the smoke into his lungs and ordered a large whisky and soda. He wondered contentedly how many of the Colonel's rules of health he would break that evening, and began to feel comfortably warm again. At dinner, he thought, he would drink a bottle of Burgundy, eat a Beef-steak Tatar, order coffee and brandy and smoke to its butt the largest and best cigar in the hotel. Blast Baxeter!

6

NEXT day the sun suddenly appeared grinning, as if to say he had only been hiding for fun. Carolus had breakfast in bed, but was down in the lounge before any of the principals had yet appeared and only a small group of companions and dependants was in evidence. Rupert Priggley rose from an armchair and came over to him.

"I know," he said, "the scene of the crime! That's where you're going this bright morning, isn't it?"

It was, and Carolus admitted it.

"Couldn't be cornier, could it? I suppose if you'd gone out on the day after the murder you'd have been looking for footprints."

"Quite likely. The police were. And found them. I'm not going to look for anything in particular, but I would like to see the place. It's four miles out on the Lilbourne road."

They climbed into the Bentley Continental and left the Royal Hydro, grey and grandiose even on that cheerful morning.

"I must say I've never known you take a case so casually," remarked Rupert. "It must have been days before you began at all and now you don't seem properly steamed up. Yet it's a pretty brutal thing."

"I don't feel any responsibility, this time," said Carolus.

"John Moore's in charge and he's perfectly able to do the job. At present I'm almost dabbling."

The banks between which they ran were yellow with primroses and at one point they could see stretching between the trees the haze of bluebells.

After three miles Carolus began to drive slowly, looking for the quarry on his left. They nearly missed it, for the cart-track leading to it was half-hidden by the bursting bushes.

"This is where the car must have stood—just off the verge, because it left no tyre-marks."

"Do you suppose it was her car?"

"Probably but there's no certainty of that. No one seems to have seen it. Yet that cottage overlooks the spot."

"So the body was dragged from here to the quarry?"

"Apparently, yes. Quite a distance, but she wasn't a heavy woman. One thing is quite certain—it was carefully planned. The murderer must have brought his props with him unless . . . let's go across to that cottage."

It was a small double-fronted cottage and a brick path led up to its front door. This did not look as though it had been opened for years and the windows to right and left of it, with lace curtains and plants in them, looked hermetically sealed. Carolus knocked, but there was no response. He tried again, and was about to turn away when he saw that a tall angular woman had appeared from the back of the premises and was watching him in sullen silence.

"Yes?" she said.

Her dark hair hung untidily round her face and she wore an apron of sacking. A forbidding-looking woman.

"I'm sorry to trouble you . . ." began Carolus.

"It's the murder again, is it? I thought I'd done with that. What do you want this time? I've got my washing to do."

She spoke in a raw aggrieved voice, yet there was something suggesting that under her surly manner she was not as unfriendly as she seemed.

"I wondered if I might ask you a few questions, Mrs . . ."

"Goggs. I suppose you can. There's no law against asking questions, is there? You better come in, only you'll have to come the back way. Mind that bucket."

She led them into one of the front rooms, which was so dark that it took Carolus a few moments to find his way to the chair she indicated. The room smelt of cheese, soap, damp and flower-pots, with a faint faraway odour of ancient meals.

"Yes, I didn't think I'd have any more of it," said Mrs Goggs, "not after the questions they asked last time. Anyone would think I'd done for the poor woman myself or my husband had. What is it you want to know?"

"First of course, did you hear anything that night?"

"No. Only the dog."

"The dog?"

"Yes. Don't you know about that? I told all the others. We were sitting in the kitchen at the time . . ."

"*What* time?"

"Don't ask me that. It's years since we've had a clock in the house, though my husband's never been late for his work. He works for Mr Raydell, the farmer at Lilbourne, and he seems to know by instink when it's time to get up in the morning. Winter and summer it's the same. Our old clock went wrong ever so long ago and I've never bothered. So I can't tell you what time it was we heard that dog."

"But approximately?"

"We were just thinking about going to bed. Somewhere round about nine, I daresay. Only don't take me up on that."

"Was it very unusual to hear a dog barking?"

"Certainly it was. There isn't a house for half a mile here and this dog was barking as though it was shut up. Went on, it did. I said to my husband, I said, 'I wonder

57

whatever that is?' He said it must be someone out in the road with a dog. Well, we get them stopping along this road in cars at night. You wouldn't believe they could be that shameless. I don't know, I'm sure."

"So you thought it was a dog belonging to someone in a car?"

"Well, what else was there to think? I said to my husband, 'You better go out and see what's the matter,' I said, but he wasn't having any of that. Why should he, that's what I say. We weren't to know someone was being strangulated not a stone's throw away, were we? Anyway, there it was. After a time the barking stopped."

"Did you hear a car drive away?"

"Well, we wouldn't, would we? Not with them passing all the time. We never even knew one had stopped, to tell you the truth, though we might have guessed it from this dog barking."

"When did you first know about the murder?"

"Not till halfway through the next morning. It was Thickett found her and of course he wouldn't say anything to us."

"Oh. Why not?"

"We weren't speaking. Hadn't been for a long time. Well, I wouldn't demean myself. Not with all I know about him. Must be more than a year since we haven't spoken. So he wouldn't say anything to us. It was the police came and told me first, wanting to know what I knew about it. They'd taken the poor lady away by then, so I never saw the way she was laid out, but from all accounts it was enough to upset anyone, lying there as though she was waiting to be measured up."

"Thickett's the roadmender, I believe?"

"That's what he calls himself, but by what I can hear he may not be much longer now the Council's got to know about him."

"Where does he live?"

"Right the other side of Buddington, but if you want to see him he'll be in the Star at Lilbourne at twelve o'clock. He always takes his bit of dinner in there, such as she gives him, though from all accounts she's too busy running down to the Bottle and Jug near where she lives to think about giving him a proper dinner. Anyway, he always takes it into the Star as regularly as clockwork and has it with a pint of mild, that's why my husband won't go there mid-day. So if you want to see him about anything, there you are."

"Thank you, Mrs Goggs."

On the way to the car, Rupert, who had remained silent during this interrogation, grinned broadly.

"I thought at first she was going to make a nice suspect," he said. "Looked it, didn't she? But she turned out to be just as garrulous as all the rest of them. Pity, really."

Carolus said nothing. But in a moment he stopped and turned back.

"Mrs Goggs!" he called.

The woman appeared again.

"What is it this time?" she asked. "Anyone would think I've got nothing to do."

"Do you grow lilies in your garden?"

"Lilies? You mean the big white ones?"

"Yes."

"What they call Madonna lilies, you mean?"

"That's it."

"Or some people call them Easter lilies because they come early?"

"Do they? I daresay. Do you grow them?"

"No. I can't say I do," said Mrs Goggs regretfully. "She'd got some in her hands, hadn't she? So they told me. No. My husband won't have anything like that. He says it makes him think of funerals. Well, it does, doesn't it? And the smell. Still there you are."

This time Carolus reached the car.

"The Star at Lilbourne I take it?" said Rupert. "I might have known. There's always a pub in your cases. I believe you like all that phony darts-with-the-locals stuff. Personally, it makes me sick to my stomach. Hacking jackets and pipes and patronizing shove ha'penny."

"I just want some information," said Carolus mildly. "And you've heard where we shall find Thickett."

"If he turns out to be a picturesque gaffer with an accent like a BBC rustic and a clay pipe, I shall walk straight out."

But Thickett was not like that. He was ginger-haired and had a fine glossy moustache. He sat bolt upright at a white scrubbed table in the clean little public bar of the Star, and eyed Carolus and Rupert with solemn curiosity. The landlord, a jolly little man, served them with bitter and seemed about to start a cheerful conversation when Carolus turned to the roadmender.

"Mr Thickett?"

"That's my name."

"Mine's Deene. I'm trying to find out something about the death of Miss Carew."

Mr Thickett sat still, eyeing Carolus without hostility but as though he needed to hear more before speaking.

"I'm acting for her cousin, Miss Tissot."

Still there was no response from Thickett.

"I understand you found the body?"

"In my humble calling," pronounced Mr Thickett with no humility in his manner, "I am accustomed to finding all sorts of things left by the roadside."

"Not corpses, surely?" put in Rupert Priggley.

"Not necessarily corpses," agreed Mr Thickett, "but all sorts of things."

"The body of Miss Carew was not by the roadside, was it?"

"No," conceded Thickett, "because it had been dragged into the quarry. Otherwise it would have been."

"Think so?"

"Stands to reason. Where were the shoes they found? Where was the hat?"

"What hat?"

Thickett eyed him triumphantly.

"Oh you don't know about the hat?"

"No."

"There was a woman's hat on the ground."

"Where?"

"Between the road and the quarry."

"Whose was it?"

"Miss Carew's. What do you think of that?"

"Not much. Rather natural isn't it, if she was dragged across? Her hat fell off in the process."

"You don't think much of that? All I can say is, the police investigating thought a lot of it. A lot of it, they thought, when I told them."

It seemed that Mr Thickett was not impressed by Carolus as an investigator.

"Then what about the lilies?" asked Mr Thickett.

"What about them?"

"They were in her hands."

"I know."

"Perhaps you don't think much of *them*?"

"How many were there?"

Mr Thickett stared at Carolus, blinked twice, and said—"What do you mean?"

"How many stems were there?"

"One."

"How many flowers on it?"

"That's funny," said Mr Thickett seriously. "You don't think much of the hat but you want to know how many flowers there were. As if it made any difference."

"It makes every difference."

Mr Thickett considered.

"If it makes every difference I have no objection to telling you. In my station in life I'm considered to be a very observant man. The police said to me themselves, 'If you hadn't noticed what you did, Mr Thickett, I don't know where we should be'. Miss Carew might have been lying out there to this day. I might not have had to spend a day at the inquest."

"Do you remember how many there were?"

"Three," said Mr Thickett. "If it's of any interest to you. There was three. No more and no less. I can answer for it. But where does that come in?"

As though rather baffled by that question Carolus hurriedly asked another.

"How did she look? The dead woman, I mean?"

"Horrible," said Mr Thickett.

"Do you mean the expression on her face?"

"That's just what I do mean. It was horrible. In my simple way of life I have become accustomed to seeing things that would upset most people. I was first on the scene when there was that car smash last year and three died outright and the other later in hospital. Scarcely recognizable they were. But it didn't turn me up like this did."

"What kind of expression?"

"What *kind* of expression? What kind of expression would you expect anyone to have when they'd just been strangled? It was horrible. I can't say more than that. Horrible. As if the eyes were popping out of her head and her mouth wide open."

"You were very upset?"

"I'm not easily put out, but yes I *was* upset that morning."

"Yet you did not go to the cottage a few yards away?"

"Goggses? No."

"Why not?" asked Carolus mischievously.

"In my calling," said Thickett, "I have to get used to abuse and slander. There's always someone ready to say you're not doing your job properly. But when it comes to taking anyone's character away, well. That's all I can say."

"So you went to the call-box?"

"I did. And in a few minutes the police were on the spot. I will say that. They did not waste any time. Almost the first words they said to me were—'It's a good thing you found it, Thickett.' And it was a good thing, when you come to look at it. Otherwise them that did it would never be found."

"Why do you say 'them'? Do you think there was more than one?"

"I shouldn't be surprised. If you'd seen the expression on her face."

"But if there had been more than one wouldn't they have carried the body instead of dragging it?"

"Unless one of them was to have stayed in the car."

"In that case the dog would have been quietened, surely?"

"Oh, I don't know anything about that," said Thickett severely. "I believe there was some story told about a dog barking, but was it a reliable Source where that came from? That's the question."

Carolus invited Thickett to drink and the roadmender agreed to a pint as though he were making a concession. The landlord, who had never moved from behind his bar, took no part in the conversation to which he listened avidly.

"Then," said Mr. Thickett, "there's the question of Compensation." Carolus showed that he did not understand. "For me. For finding it."

"I don't quite see . . ."

"Nerves," explained Mr Thickett with an altogether new enthusiasm. "Nerves. All shattered to pieces. Insom . . . can't sleep at night. Nightmares."

"I understood you to say that in your calling . . ."

"Not corpses, we don't reckon on. Not with expressions like that to haunt you for the rest of your life."

"What about the National Health? Doesn't that provide for the after-effects of corpse-finding?"

"I shall have to see about it, I suppose. Unless the relatives act as they should. It's upset my wife, too. She says she can't hardly bear me coming home in the evening for fear I've found another one."

"That's surely not very likely?"

"You never know. In my calling . . ."

"An occupational hazard, you think? At all events I'm much obliged to you, Mr Thickett." Carolus passed him a pound note which disappeared as though a conjuror had held it. "You've been most helpful."

"Did She tell you where to find me?"

Carolus, who was accustomed to meet pronouns unrelated and incorporate, appearing from nowhere, as it were, was somewhat at a loss this time.

"Her near the quarry," explained Thickett, unable to pronounce the name.

"As a matter of fact she did," said Carolus.

"I thought so. It only shows."

"She also said you were clever, Mr Thickett."

"That's no compliment coming from her. I make no claims to cleverness or anything else. It wouldn't do in my walk of life."

"Did you know the other murdered woman?"

"I attend St Augustine's church," said Mr Thickett, "so I could scarcely help knowing her by sight, could I? Poor lady, I'm told she looked as horrible as the one I found. What kind of a madman would do a thing like that, I should like to know?"

"Not mad," said Carolus, "clever."

He left Thickett staring up over his tankard.

7

"It's all very interesting," said Rupert Priggley over lunch "and I've no doubt you're beginning to 'see light' or 'form the first vague idea', or whatnot. But you must admit you're being rather leisurely about it."

"I'm on holiday. Recovering from an illness."

"Oh phoo-ee. If you thought there was any urgency you'd be leaping about in disguise or tearing round cross-examining people like a lunatic. I suppose you've got your reason for playing it slow. Or is it the effect of this town?"

Carolus took a glance round the dining-room. It was the briskest scene of the day at the Royal Hydro.

"After all, it's quite a lurid little affair," went on Rupert. "Two elderly ladies, whose only offence appears to be that they had a lot of money, strangled in the same night and in the same district. You can't call it dull, can you? Yet here you are, asking a few questions, interviewing a few people who even you could scarcely call suspects . . ."

"I don't see why not."

"Mrs Goggs? Thickett in his humble calling? The Baxeters? Come now, sir."

"Who would you say was a suspect?"

"Well, anyone in the town, I suppose."

"Why limit it to the town? There's the man who bought gold from each of the two women. He lives in London. No, Rupert. You've missed the whole point."

"Go on. I'll buy it. I'll be Doctor Watson. What's the whole point?"

"This case is unique in my experience. In every other murder case I've ever touched the motive has been clear and I've had to look for suspects. In this I've got my suspects and cannot for the life of me understand the motive."

"Money, surely."

"How? No one benefits from the death of both women."

"I see what you mean. What do we do, then? Bash on regardless?"

"Exactly. Routine enquiries. You'll find it will take shape."

"Who is next?"

"A bootmaker called Humpling."

The shop was a small one-room affair and its proprietor, a thin and nervous-looking man whose face wore a perpetually crestfallen expression, was at work in it. Carolus explained his business.

"Oh dear," said the bootmaker in a somewhat whining voice. "I've told the police all I know. It seems very hard that I should have to go over it again."

"You don't *have* to," said Carolus. "You can refuse to tell me anything at all."

"It's the Time it takes," moaned Mr Humpling.

"You could go on working surely?"

"Let's get it over with. What do you want to know?"

"About that pair of shoes that were found near Miss Carew's body."

"I'd repaired them. Never mind how I know. There's a way I have of putting two tacks in together so that I can always tell a pair of shoes I've repaired. I knew I'd done these."

"Recently?"

"They'd scarcely been worn from the time I had done them."

"But you've no means of knowing when that was?"

"No, I haven't. Might have been any time. I've had this shop for nearly twenty years." He broke off to answer a woman at the counter. "No, they're not ready," he said. "I'll try and finish them by tomorrow." The woman expressed her annoyance and went. "See? They're on at you the whole time. Don't seem to understand there's others to be done."

66

"Must be very tiring," said Carolus soothingly.

"It's not the work, it's the people. I'd work all right if they'd only leave me in peace. I've only got one pair of hands. I told one the other day, I'm not an Indian goddess, I said. What more do you want to know so that I can get on?"

"A pair of shoes was missing from here, wasn't it?"

"One. In all the time I've been here."

"When did that happen?"

"About six months ago. Some time before Christmas. They belonged to a man called Purley, who has left the district. The fuss he made you'd have thought they was solid gold. You see I used to keep the shoes that were ready on a rack by the counter. I've altered it since this happened. Anyone could have reached across when I wasn't looking, and that's what must have happened."

"You don't think it was the pair the police found?"

"It could have been, I suppose. I'm not to know, really. They were size eight, anyway."

"You've no suspicion as to who could have taken them?"

"I told the police I hadn't. But since then I've come to remember. There was that artist chap who called about that time."

"Who was that?"

"I don't know his name. He brought a pair of shoes to be repaired."

"How do you know he was an artist?"

"You could tell. He wore a big black hat and a cape."

"A beard, of course?"

"No. I don't think he had a beard. But dark glasses; I remember those."

"What makes you think he had anything to do with the shoes?"

"I didn't like the look of him and it was about the same time. There was something funny about him. Besides, I'd

67

never seen him before and haven't since. All the others who came at that time were regulars."

"Five good reasons, but not quite enough to convict your artist."

"No. I don't want to convict anyone, but I'm sure it was him took those shoes."

"Do you know a painter called Johnson? Mr Ben Johnson?"

"Him? It wasn't him. I knew him when he used to bring me shoes that hadn't much left of them to repair. That was in the old days, before he was famous. It's different now. But he never dresses himself up in big hats and that."

"You're convinced your man was a stranger?"

"Yes."

"I won't keep you from your work then, Mr Humpling. And I won't trouble you again."

"That's all right. Only it's the Time. Someone will be on at me for not having their shoes ready."

From the shop Carolus turned towards the centre of the little town. Buddington did not cover a large area and to Rupert's disgust Carolus had left his car at the hotel.

"Where now?" sighed Rupert. "This foot-slogging is killing me."

"I want to see the lady who lost her lilies."

"A pretty piece of alliteration, but what do you really think you'll gain by it? However, let's do another mile or two's tramp."

"It's not far. Nothing is in Buddington. Primrose Cottage, 77 Station Road, is the address."

"And the name?"

"Gosport. Mrs Gosport."

They found her at home. Station Road was a long street of identical red brick houses with small gardens in front of them. The street led from the station to Market Street, itself a turning off the Promenade, the principal street of the town. Primrose Cottage was at the Market Street end, so that it was not far from the Granodeon Cinema, and the Dragon Hotel. For that matter it was not far from Dehra Dun and Rossetti Lodge, or from any other point in Buddington.

Mrs Gosport was a neat and beady-eyed little woman who received them with a smile, the first they had been given by anyone they had interrogated.

"You can see where they were taken from, can't you?" she said pointing to the stumps from which two *candida* lilies had been cut. "It was a shame, because they weren't fully out and I always give them to St Augustine's, which is the church I go to. Two they took, and they were going to be a picture. Well, you can see from the rest."

"You've never lost anything from the garden before?"

"Not to mention, I haven't. I once caught the little girl next door picking one of my cornflowers, but that was a long time ago and she wanted it for a botany class. I told her she should have Asked, that's all. They're wonderful smelling, my lilies. The lady next door says she can smell them all over the house."

"You know that lilies were found on the two bodies, don't you?"

"That's just it. Some people think they were mine, but of course you can't be sure. There's others grow lilies in the town, though not to come up to mine. There's Smitherses the nurserymen, though Mr Smithers himself said to me, 'We can't grow lilies like yours, Mrs Gosport.'"

"The police seem to believe they were yours, anyway."

"I've heard they do but they've never been to see me about it. I went round and reported it on the morning after they'd gone and the Sergeant said they'd do everything they could. I didn't know about the murders then, you see. But those investigating haven't troubled to come and see me, though they went twice to Mrs Plummer's."

"Oh. Why?"

69

"She's supposed to have seen something on the night. She lives right opposite to where Mrs Westmacott lived, though I don't believe she knew the poor lady more than by sight."

"You knew Mrs Westmacott?"

"She came to St Augustine's where I go and I saw her every Sunday. But no. The police haven't asked me anything. Too busy listening to what Mrs Plummer had to tell them about a stranger going to the house that night. It makes you wonder, doesn't it?"

"It certainly does," said Carolus truthfully. "Have you any idea what time your lilies were stolen?"

"Not really. They were there when I came in from the pictures at six o'clock and when I went to the door in the morning they'd gone. That's all I know. My sister who lives with me's a ninvalide, and sleeps in the front, but she never heard anything."

"Wouldn't the thief have been seen?"

"Not if he was careful. We're farthest away from a street lamp here and it's dark at night. He could have nipped in the gate and popped out again without anyone knowing anything about it."

"I expect that's what he did."

"I'm glad you came and asked me about it. You'd have thought the police would have done, wouldn't you? After finding them on the bodies and that. But no. They've time to see that Mrs Plummer, asking her all sorts of questions, so the lady next door to her told me, but not to come here. You can't help thinking, can you?"

"No," said Carolus.

He could see that reiteration was about to set in and prepared to take his leave. Not liking to ask any precise directions, he intended to find the home of Mrs Plummer by enquiries on the spot. But Mrs Gosport voiced the suggestion herself.

"I should go and see her if I was you," she said bitterly.

"And hear whatever it was kept her talking to them for an hour or more. You can tell her you've been to see me about the lilies, then she'll know she's not the only one with information."

"Thank you. Which is her house?"

"House? She hasn't got a house and never has had that I remember. She's a caretaker, so-called, for the house opposite Westmacotts'. Charlton, its name is, a big grey house. You can't miss it. Yes. You tell her I had some information for you. She won't like that."

"If by any chance you should lose any more lilies, will you let me know at once? My name's Deene and I'm staying at the Royal Hydro."

"Yes. Certainly I will. That's a promise."

Carolus was so sure Mrs Plummer would not like references to Mrs Gosport that he kept the source of his information about her till he had heard what Mrs Plummer had to say. She was, unexpectedly, a jovial-looking person who invited him into Charlton as though it was rather a joke. Indeed, in appearance it was, a huge house like a commercial hotel in the Midlands, leather armchairs, Turkey carpets, ponderous furniture and brassware. They went to the dining-room, which had a mahogany table capable of seating twelve large persons and a sideboard with an array of giant electro-plated dish-covers.

"Well!" said Mrs Plummer cheerfully. "You want to know what I know about the murder opposite, do you? I'm not surprised, because as far as anyone can tell I saw the murderer. What do you think of that?"

"Very interesting," said Carolus inadequately.

"I can tell you the time and everything."

"Can you indeed?"

"Yes. It was just gone eleven."

"What was?"

"When I saw this man. My husband had gone to bed. He's a fitter at the gasworks and I always say it makes him sleepy. 'I think I'll go up,' he said as soon as he'd finished his supper. Or rather down, because we sleep in the basement. He won't even sit up ten minutes for the telly. It's bed for him as soon as ever he can. I switched off at eleven o'clock, because there was boxing coming on, which I don't like. Then I went to the front door to let the dog out."

"That would be about five past eleven?"

"Just about. I was standing there waiting for the dog and thinking it was chilly and I'd better leave him out for a minute when this man came along."

"Which man?" Carolus couldn't refrain from asking.

"This man I'm telling you about. He gave me quite a turn."

"Why?"

"There was something funny about him. Big black hat like Guy Fawkes. A long black sort of cape. Dark glasses. I stood there watching, ready to slam the door to if he was to come anywhere near. He went right up the steps of the house opposite, where Mrs Westmacott lived."

"Did you notice whether he hesitated at all, Mrs Plummer? Or did he walk straight up as though he knew the house?"

"I can't say I noticed him hesitating. No, he went straight up the steps. It seemed late for anyone to be going there, but they're funny people the Westmacotts and I didn't think much about it till afterwards. Of course when I heard what had happened I told the police."

"You didn't wait to see him let into the house, then?"

"No. I wished I had of done. But the dog ran in past me and I didn't want to catch my death of cold."

"It's a pity we don't know who let him in. If he was let in."

"Well, of course he was. He murdered her, didn't he?"

"He may not have been admitted at all. And if he was, there is no certainty that he was responsible for the death of Mrs Westmacott. Was he carrying anything?"

"Not that I noticed."

"No lilies, for instance?"

"Lilies?" Mrs Plummer laughed. "Oh, you've been listening to old Gosport, have you? She's got lilies on the brain."

"All the same two of hers were stolen that evening. And both the dead women had lilies in their hands."

"I daresay. But what does she know about it? The police haven't even been to see her."

"You saw no lilies, anyway?"

"I didn't. But there was no telling what he may have had under that big cloak of his, was there? He could have carried all the lilies *she* could grow and no one would be any the wiser."

"You had never seen this visitor before?"

"Never. There's plenty of funny people used to go to the house, but I'd never seen him."

Carolus thanked Mrs Plummer, and resisting the temptation to look under the dish-covers followed her from the dining-room. At the front door he paused.

"Yes, you can see the entrance clearly enough," he remarked.

"It's lit up at night by that street-lamp right over it."

"Could he see you, do you think?"

"I should doubt it. Our people don't like these bushes cut and as you see they screen us off a bit. Besides, he had those dark glasses on, like a blind man with a collecting-box."

Rupert Priggley fell into step with Carolus as they walked away.

"That's quite enough for this afternoon, surely, sir? I feel as though I was on a route march."

"I thought I was being leisurely?"

"Yes, but do let's keep our sense of proportion. There's no need to rush at it."

"You can have an hour's break," said Carolus grimly,

"but at six o'clock sharp we go to the bar of the Dragon. I want to get there at opening time."

"Who do we meet there?"

"Almost everyone of any importance in the case, I hope."

Rupert sighed noisily.

"I almost wish I'd gone to Cornwall with the Holling-bournes," he said.

8

THAT evening at the Dragon changed the whole aspect of the matter, for during the course of it Carolus realized that the double murder at Buddington could no longer be regarded as a pleasant holiday task, a problem to be solved at leisure, something to occupy him during convalescence. He was up against intelligence, desperate cunning and a kind of diabolic nerve. Carolus saw that unless he discovered the whole truth and acted promptly a particularly vile murder might go unpunished, for, able and resourceful as John Moore was, there were methods the police could not use and they might well be those necessary here.

Besides, during that evening Carolus met a number of people whose connections with the case would seem to be a good deal closer than those of persons who had merely seen or heard something on the night. He learned, moreover, some surprising facts. In a word, it was that evening at the Dragon which brought him to himself, which made him cease to be a dilettante playing round with sometimes irrelevant questions, and turned him into the Carolus of other grim and ugly occasions when he had had to show courage and energy as well as his gift for problem-solving.

But the change in Carolus was an inward one. It was once said of him that his reason for investigating murder was that it was the only thing he took seriously. His debonair and flippant manner remained unchanged, but secretly he resolved that nothing, no deceit or bluff or false trail already or about to be laid, should divert him. Whatever it cost him in time, health or energy, in concentrated angry thought or deliberate outward hypocrisy, he would solve this thing. He recognized a challenge, he saw that imagination and intelligence had been used and an elaborate network of deceit was there to entrap him. There was nothing slapdash or impulsive in the way the two women had been killed. If ever there was a calculated crime, this was it. Carolus realized that it called for equally calculating and ruthless methods of investigation.

The afternoon ended as trivially as it had begun. At teatime he approached Miss Tissot. It was a busy hour at the Royal Hydro, for the guests had been nearly three hours without food and eyed with anxious avidity the trays brought to them in the Palm Lounge. Neat but satisfying sandwiches, heavily buttered crumpets and a selection of creamy cakes were set before each of the guests, and a party of foreigners near Carolus watched with wonder as the elderly English disposed of them. They had heard of the English having meals between meals, but they had never seen them in action.

Miss Tissot was not behind her fellow-guests in this, but looked up from the manipulation of a particularly well-buttered crumpet when Carolus introduced Rupert Priggley.

"Priggley?" she said, lifting her nostrils as though the word denoted a bad smell. "What a very unfortunate name!"

"Italian derivation," improvised Rupert, who had learned something of Miss Tissot from Carolus. "The original form was Parri-Galli. There was a Cardinal Parri-

Galli who was an enemy of the Borgias. His brother, my ancestor, escaped to England and, embracing Protestantism, anglicized his name. The present Conte de Parri-Galli lives in San Remo."

Miss Tissot's nostrils were lowered somewhat and Carolus took advantage of this to warn her that the Baxeters were hoping to make her acquaintance. After all, they were fellow beneficiaries under Miss Carew's will.

"I trust nothing of the sort will be necessary," said Miss Tissot. "It would be most distasteful to receive persons of their type. It is bad enough to find myself cheek by jowl with the riff-raff in this hotel. . . ." She stared ferociously at a colonial bishop and his family and let her gaze dwell on a Q.C. famous for his successful prosecutions in cases of fraud. "These Baxeters, I understand, belong to some disreputable religious persuasion and hold nameless orgies in enclosed areas of woodland."

"They are Pantheists and practise nudism," admitted Carolus, "but I imagine with the greatest of propriety."

"Vulgar," said Miss Tissot, attacking a meringue. "Small wonder my cousin met her death in that extremely plebeian way. I warned her of her folly a score of times. However, if I am forced to meet these people it need be nothing but a formality connected with my cousin's will."

Punctually at six o'clock Carolus drove up to the Dragon and parked his car.

The Dragon was for many years the principal hostelry in Buddington, but with the building of the Royal Hydro it had become a 'good-class Commercial'. It preserved its Georgian façade, on which a newly-painted sign hung under a bracket of elaborately wrought iron. In spite of the fact that it was owned by one of the big catering syndicates and managed by an Old Rugbeian it had kept something faintly Dickensian in its atmosphere. Its bar was a popular meeting-place with a clientele which Miss Shapely, who was in charge of it, called 'very mixed'.

In charge? Carolus soon found that was an understatement. Not the captain of a ship, the head prefect of a public school, the sergeant of a platoon of recruits knew an authority so absolute as hers. For fifteen years Miss Shapely had ruled it while managers came and went, scarcely presuming to look in and certainly never interfering with her.

She was a splendid woman, august and stately, who moved like a ship under sail and talked in a throaty contralto. She spoke of her domain as 'my bar' and seemed so much a part of it that she could scarcely be imagined elsewhere. Young barmen were employed to assist her, but none had lasted more than a few months and some had left after a week. She called them all Fred, ignoring any hopes they might voice of keeping their own names. If one of them, serving a customer at the far end of the bar, attempted a snatch of conversation Miss Shapely would call him briskly to another duty. It was her bar and there must be no whispered pleasantries by her assistant.

If Miss Shapely was not beloved in the town, she was revered and the favour of her smile and recognition was eagerly sought. She accepted a drink as Queen Victoria might have accepted a gift from some flamboyant and barbaric tributary. No one had ever discovered her Christian name, but that was a small matter, since the man with the courage to use it had not been born.

Carolus, entering with Rupert, found that they were the only customers.

"Good evening," he said brightly and asked for his drinks.

"Fred will serve you," announced Miss Shapely and seemed interested in far-away serious things.

How did one start, wondered Carolus, at a loss for once. Nice bar you've got here? Been a lovely day? No. Neck or nothing. He stood square in front of Miss Shapely.

"I have come to see you," he said, "on a matter of some importance."

77

Miss Shapely's eyes reluctantly met his.

"If it's anything to do with the business . . ."

"No. No. I shouldn't trouble you with that. I wanted your opinion."

"I never talk to the press," said Miss Shapely.

"Naturally not," said Carolus.

"I do not approve of opinion polls."

"Of course you don't. I entirely sympathize. I am investigating the two murders . . ."

"I couldn't give any statement to ordinary police officials. The Chief Constable is a customer of mine and if he requires any information from me he will ask for it."

Carolus was desperate. He decided on a gamble.

"No. No," he said, "you misunderstand me. I'm not a policeman. I'm investigating for Television."

He watched the effect of that magic word. Yes. It worked. Miss Shapely smiled.

"I see," she said. It was not effusive, but it was enough.

"We are organizing a programme. We need your assistance, Miss Shapely."

"It depends. I couldn't allow anything of that sort in my bar, of course."

"No. It was your personal co-operation I was hoping to obtain."

"I do not often have an opportunity of seeing television programmes," said Miss Shapely, "but such as I have seen have been most interesting."

"May I ask you a few questions? Then I can get an idea of how to arrange the programme. I feel it should be built round you."

"Certainly," beamed Miss Shapely.

"I understand that Charles Carew comes here?"

Miss Shapely sighed.

"He is not exactly the type of customer I seek to encourage," she said. "I never allow any language in my bar and

78

have had to Speak To Mr Carew more than once. But he certainly comes in here."

"Will I see him this evening?"

"He usually comes in at about seven and again at nine."

"Not in the mornings?"

"Very seldom. The last occasion on which he came in during the morning was about a week before the murders. I remember it because I had some Trouble that day."

"Really? With Carew?"

"Oh no. I should never have any trouble with him. He would be Asked To Leave at once. No. This was with a farmer named Raydell. Usually a very quiet and respectful man. On that occasion he abused his position."

"How?"

"He took a liberty which I could never permit."

"No!"

"A quite unforgivable liberty. I had to be firm."

"I hope he didn't . . ."

"He brought a wild animal into my bar."

"A wild animal?"

"Yes. A creature resembling a small leopard. He called it an ocelot."

"Good heavens!"

"You may well say that. It wasn't only the impudence of it, it was the sly way he did it. He waited till my back was turned. Nobody saw it as he led it in on a chain. The first to see it was old Mr Sawyer, one of my very best customers. He suddenly found the thing sniffing at him. He does like a drop of gin, I won't deny, and just recently has been a little liberal with himself. When this creature appeared to him he thought . . . it seems he occasionally suffered from delusions after spells of over-indulgence. He dropped his glass and fell into convulsions. When I glanced over and saw what had caused it I . . . fortunately I did not quite swoon, but I was not myself. For the first time in the fifteen years I have been in charge of this bar I was unnerved. A

79

lady in the corner began to scream. It was a most scandalous scene. Nothing like it had ever taken place while I have been here.

"Then Mr Raydell instead of instantly taking the creature out began to explain that it was quite harmless and slept on his bed. 'Mr Raydell,' I said, 'you will please remove that beast at once and never bring it into my bar again. I'm surprised at you doing such a thing.' 'It's only an ocelot,' he said. '*Only* an ocelot—that's quite enough, I should think,' I told him. 'If you don't take it away immediately I shall call the police. I won't have ocelots in my bar!' 'There's only one,' said Mr Raydell. 'I don't care if there is one or fifty,' I told him. 'It's the principle of the thing. Now take it away at once, please. Suppose it went for anybody? It might kill some poor old lady before you could stop it.' "

"Who was in the bar at the time?"

"Oh, a number of people. It was my busy time. Mr and Mrs Baxeter were present. They do not often come in and never have anything but Lemon Barley, but they happened to be here. Then Mr Bickley who worked for Mrs Westmacott. As I say, Mr Carew. There was Mr Gilling who looks after the car-park at the Granodeon Cinema, a very quiet respectable person; also a chauffeur from the Royal Hydro named Wright."

"Splendid collection. Anyone else?"

"Yes, unfortunately. One of my Crosses. Mr Ben Johnson, an artist. There was the lady who screamed, with her husband, but they were just passing through and staying in the hotel."

"And they all heard you say that about killing an old lady?"

"When I mean my voice to be heard it *is* heard."

"So Mr Raydell went off?"

"At once. Yes. But I was upset. I didn't show it, but I was very upset indeed."

"I'm not surprised. Mr Raydell is a familiar figure in the town?"

"Oh yes. He's a farmer in quite a big way. Everyone knows him and until this occasion he had never given me any cause for offence. His farm is well known, because he has some successful dairy cattle, or something of the sort. I understand they have taken prizes for the quantity of milk they have given. Someone explained it one evening, but I had to discourage the topic. It did not sound very nice . . ."

"Now tell me about Mr Ben Johnson, Miss Shapely. Do you think he would fit into the programme?"

"Not if I'm in it. I couldn't possibly appear with Mr Johnson. He is a most violent and self-assertive man. His Language is dreadful. He drinks more than is good for him. I have heard things about his private life which are shameful. Quite shameful. I have begged him not to come here, but it's no use. On more than one occasion I have had to put him in his place for familiarity."

"I gather he wasn't fond of the Westmacotts?"

"He spoke disgracefully about them. I've heard him call Mrs Westmacott awful names."

"No. Really?"

"Yes. He didn't know her, but it seems she had wished to befriend him. 'The old . . .' (you know what I mean), he shouted. For a long time Mr Johnson was unsuccessful as an artist. No one was prepared to buy the pictures he painted and I must say I wasn't surprised. I don't know much about art, but I do like a picture to look like what it says it is. Years ago, before Mr Johnson had been taken up, he brought one of his paintings in here. He wanted me to hang it up and try to sell it. It was a most peculiar picture which I thought represented a tropical bird in a cage. I asked him what he called it and he said it did not matter much. 'Fresh herrings,' he said. 'No, call it Nude Figure. They like that better.' Of course as soon as he said that I told him to take the thing away. But you see the kind of artist he is. While he was unable to sell his pictures he did not come to the notice of Mrs Westmacott, but after people began to buy them and he became known, Mrs Westmacott wished to meet him. He spoke in the most dreadful way of her. He said he would never so-and-so well meet her . . ."

"So-and-so?"

"Beginning with B," explained Miss Shapely. "Oh he never went farther than that. I had to speak to him. 'Language, Mr Johnson, language!' I said to warn him. Then I pointed out that he did not even know Mrs Westmacott. 'Never set eyes on the old . . .' "

"Yes?"

"He used a disgraceful word."

"Beginning with B?"

"Certainly not! Not in my bar. He called her . . . I scarcely like to say it . . . he actually called her a cow. 'Never set eyes on her, nor she on me. And never likely to.' You see the kind of man he is? He had no consideration for the family. Spoke most disrespectfully of Mr Gabriel Westmacott."

"Why?"

"Mr Gabriel Westmacott is a well known lecturer."

"I must say I had never heard of him."

"Oh yes. Only a fortnight ago the *Buddington Courier* published an announcement that he was going up to Lancashire to lecture on the following Thursday. We all read that."

"All?"

"All my regulars. It was handed round. I particularly remembered it afterwards, because the lecture was on the night his poor mother was murdered. Mr Johnson was quite violent about it. The school of art on which Mr Gabriel Westmacott lectured was not at all one he liked, it seemed."

At this moment the first of Miss Shapely's regular

customers arrived, an elderly gentleman who stumped in and asked for a double gin and soda. Miss Shapely served him herself with a queenly smile.

"There you are, Mr Sawyer. You well this evening?"

"As well as can be expected after that shock," said Mr Sawyer.

"There! That's weeks ago now, you know. You should forget it."

"What did he call it?"

"An ocelot."

Mr Sawyer turned to Carolus.

"What would you say to an ocelot attacking you in a bar in England?" he asked stertorously.

"I shouldn't speak to it," said Carolus.

"Um," said Mr Sawyer and swallowed his gin.

"Why, what did you say?"

"Um," repeated Mr Sawyer, then turning to Miss Shapely demanded another gin.

"One thing," said Miss Shapely, "you'll never see it again. Mr Raydell knows better than that. Not in my bar, anyway." Suddenly the richness left her voice and the brightness went from her eyes as another customer entered. "Good evening," she murmured disagreeably in answer to his greeting. "Fred will serve you, Mr Carew."

9

CAROLUS examined the much-discussed Charlie Carew, police suspect number one, beneficiary from the will of Sophia Carew, bankrupt reprobate with a motive for murdering his aunt. He saw a man such as one expects to see on most nights of the week in the hotel bar of any provincial town. Carew looked good-natured, waggish, not very intelligent and given to regular but not extreme over-indulgence. He would talk, one knew before hearing him, of cricket in the summer and football in the winter or, all the year round, of greyhound racing, television, horse-racing, what happened to him that morning, what he had dreamt last night, what somebody had said to him, the weather, football pools, the intelligence of his dog if he had one, the number of cigarettes he smoked and any ailments from which he might be suffering.

Miss Shapely, so far from effecting an introduction, seemed determined to ignore Carew's presence and became closely interested in Mr Symonds. But no introduction was necessary.

"Good evening," said Carew. "What did you think of the fight last night?"

For one moment Carolus wondered whether Miss Shapely had had more Trouble in her bar. But he remembered in time that another white hope of British boxing had faded.

"Tough," said Carolus. "Your name's Carew, isn't it? I have been asked by Miss Tissot to try to clear up the double murder."

Carew smiled.

"I'm your man," he said. "The odds are about three to one on. My Aunt Sophia left me her money. I haven't an alibi for that evening. I'm obviously a desperate sort of villain, anyway."

"Have a drink?" asked Carolus.

"I won't say no. Mine's a rum and Coca-Cola."

"I beg your pardon?"

"Rum and coke. Nice drink. Refreshing and potent. . . . Cheerio."

"Where were you that night, Mr Carew?"

"Looked in here about seven. I wasn't here long. Just

to wet my whistle. It was a dull sort of a day and I felt bloody tired."

"Language, Mr Carew!" called Miss Shapely imperiously.

"Then I came back as usual, didn't I, Miss Shapely? Night of the murder, remember?"

"Rather later than usual. It wasn't far short of closing time when you got back."

"Where had you been in the meantime?"

"Home, old man. Back to my little place for a snack. I always make a point of that. Doesn't do to drink unless you eat something."

"Where is your house?"

"Know the Granodeon? Not far from there. Up the back. Number 7 Quincey Street."

"You live there alone?"

"Yes, thank God. Wife and I agreed to differ some years ago and I look after myself. I don't like digs."

"Pity, though, from one point of view. It means you have no alibi for your aunt's murder."

"I know. Awkward, isn't it? But do they know what time poor old Sophia was done for? Because I may have an alibi. I was here about this time and don't suppose I left till nearly eight. Then I was back at half-past nine. It doesn't leave a lot of time."

"It didn't need a lot of time."

"But listen . . . what did you say your name was? But listen, Deene, does anyone seriously think I murdered Sophia? It's so far-fetched that I can't believe I'm really suspected."

"I should think the police have serious suspicions."

"It's quite absurd. Sophia was a dear, really. Helped me out no end of times."

"She was popular?"

"She didn't mix much here. She had friends in London. Cosmopolitan crowd—you know, talked a sort of bastard English . . ."

85

"Mr Carew!" called Miss Shapely. "Please be careful of your Language. I won't have words like that used in my bar as well you know."

"What words?" asked Carew innocently.

"You know very well. Begins with a B."

"Yes, Sophia knew any amount of foreigners. I didn't see many of them. People who had read her books. Germans, Swiss, that sort of thing. I remember there was a Doctor Fuchs . . ."

"I'm listening, Mr Carew," said Miss Shapely ominously.

"But to return to yourself," said Carolus. "Can't you produce any sort of an alibi for that hour and a half?"

"How can I have one? I was in my house frying myself a bit of steak and eating it. I'm there every evening at that time. If I had known I'd need an alibi I'd have called on the neighbours or something. But no one saw me come in or go out to the best of my knowledge."

"You see, what makes your situation so tricky is the lack of any other suspect. The only other people to benefit from your aunt's death are the Baxeters and Martha Tissot. She is physically incapable of it and the Baxeters scarcely seem . . ."

"The type? But I thought you investigators laughed at the idea of a murderous type."

"We do. But there are limits. Have you got any suggestions to make?"

"Not really. Unless it could have been someone from outside. London or somewhere. As I've told you, she had a wide acquaintance."

"You don't want me to consider *Sign of Four* sort of possibilities, do you? Someone appearing from her past with a lust for revenge. A Tuareg, perhaps?"

"No. But it needn't have been someone from Buddington. I see what you mean about the Baxeters. They don't seem exactly bloodthirsty, do they? I had dinner there once. Christ! I shall never forget it!"

"Mr Carew—Language, please," called Miss Shapely with exasperation.

"It was terrifying, old man. Positively terrifying. Beetroot and dandelion soup. Then a *hors d'oeuvres* . . ."

"Mr Carew, I shan't speak to you again!"

"Consisting of grated raw carrot and figs, followed by mock duck and sweet potatoes with semolina and fruit juice as a sweet. It turned me up, old man. The frightful thing is that Mrs Baxeter was supposed to be a wonderful cook. How can people prostitute their talents . . ."

"I shall have to ask you to leave in a minute, Mr Carew."

"Still, even offering a guest that sort of thing is not murder in the ordinary sense of the word. I had taken the trouble to buy Mrs Baxeter some flowers, too. Sorry, she said, we don't have flowers in the house. Lovely bunch of Love-Lies-Bleeding . . ."

"That's enough now, Mr Carew. You finish up your drink and leave, please. If I've told you once I've told you a thousand times I will *not* have Language."

"It was only the name of a flower."

"I daresay, but there's no need to use those words with it. Beginning with B, I mean. Well, I'll give you one more chance."

Carew looked towards the door.

"Here's old Johnson," he said. "He'll shake her. He always does."

Ben Johnson looked as though he might. His garb was an affected version of the farm-labourer's, corduroy trousers and a handkerchief knotted at the neck. He had not shaved for at least two days and whitish stubble showed on a face which looked otherwise rather young. His teeth were in urgent need of a skilled and ruthless dentist, and the hand in which he held his brandy and soda seemed a little uncertain.

"Hullo, Johnson," said Carew. "This is Carolus Deene. He's investigating the two murders."

"Evening," said the artist. "You're wasting your time. Who cares who bumped off the old crows?"

Carew giggled.

"I do rather. One was my aunt."

"Well, I know. But after a certain age what good are we to anyone? I hope when I get there someone will do me in."

"Someone probably will, if you talk like that," said Carolus. "Only a man scared of death would even do that kind of whistling in the dark."

"What in hell do you mean?"

"Er . . . Mr Johnson . . ." called Miss Shapely, mildly for such a mild expletive.

"I mean that you talk like a fool. What difference does the age of people matter when they are murdered? A murderer is arrogating to himself the powers of God. It is damnable presumption and if we, the rest of humanity, let it pass we should be pusillanimous rats. Whoever killed those women is going to pay for it with his life or liberty, I can assure you of that."

"Nice piece of tub-thumping," said the artist.

"I admit it. I just don't find murder funny, that's all. Did you know Sophia Carew?"

"Just met her. Bit of a gorgon, I thought."

"And Mrs Westmacott?"

"No, thank God. There I did draw the line. I never met that bitch . . ."

"Mr Johnson, will you please control your Language in my bar?" called Miss Shapely.

"What's the matter? I was talking about a female dog. How would you refer to it?"

"You could quite easily say a lady-dog. There's no need to use words beginning with B."

"You don't know the provocation I've had," said Ben Johnson, then turning to Carolus, Carew and Priggley went on: "You ask if I knew her. I did not, but it has cost

88

me a year's work to say so. The woman was indefatigable. She'd been patted on the head as a child by Burne-Jones or someone, and it had turned her artist-mad for the rest of her life."

"What was wrong with Burne-Jones?" asked Carolus provocatively.

"Nothing, except that he couldn't paint. A glazier . . ."

"You mean he did stained glass?"

"A paviour . . ."

"He was a mosaicist."

"A tiler, a blacksmith, a needleman, plasterer, organ-decorator, upholsterer, book-illustrator, anything you like, but don't call him an artist. As for Rossetti . . ."

"Yes?"

"Jejune. Timid. Thin," said Ben Johnson.

"Really. I'd no idea. Is that why you disliked the idea of meeting Mrs Westmacott?"

"Partly. She and her circle were still living with those old arty-crafties. But partly it was the woman's shameless persistence. She never let up. On the very evening she died I had a call from her, as you probably know."

"I didn't know. Do the police?"

"Must do. I made no secret of it at the time."

Ben Johnson looked a little uncomfortable, as though he had let out more than he meant.

"What time was it?"

"Eightish, I should say. Extraordinary. Began talking about when I should come round presently. Seemed tickled to death. Expecting me."

"What did you say?"

"I worked the old receiver gag on her. It never fails. You can buy me a drink for telling you. It'll save you quids in time and boredom. When you get some garrulous nuisance on the phone you hang up, but while *you're* talking, not while he or she is. Talkers like that never suppose that anyone will cut himself off. You remove the receiver for five minutes and you're free. It works every time and never gives offence. 'Oh but Mrs Westmacott . . .' I said that evening and bang! ended the conversation."

"Most interesting," said Carolus. "I daresay we all have occasions for that. She did not come through again?"

"No. I went out soon afterwards."

"Where?"

"None of your business."

"So you've still never seen Mrs Westmacott, nor she you?"

"Never hide nor hair, as they say. And now, what do *you* think about it?"

"I haven't got to the stage of suspicion backed with more than guesswork."

"You think it was a homicidal maniac?"

"No. I think these were carefully planned murders by person or persons with motives."

"For both?" asked Johnson sceptically. Carolus did not answer.

After a while both Johnson and Carew went to talk to others of their acquaintance. Carolus found himself alone for a moment with Priggley.

"Have you ever seen any of that man's paintings?" asked Rupert.

"No."

"God!"

Miss Shapely cleared her throat.

"It's unbelievably bad. Fetches thousands. It's the *avant-garde* of last year and there's nothing more dated than that."

"What does he paint?"

"Crucified spiders. Skulls caught in cobwebs. Tortured vultures. You know the sort of thing."

"I don't, but I'll try to guess. Now who else is there? I wonder if that farming character is here. The one with the ocelot."

Carolus leaned across the bar somewhat and asked Miss Shapely.

"Mr Raydell? Yes, that's him talking to Mr Carew. Mr Raydell! Here's a gentleman asking for you."

The farmer was as beefy and sanguine-looking as a farmer is expected to be, and seemed quite ready to talk. He had heard that Carolus was investigating the case.

"They tell me you've got an ocelot," said Carolus.

"Yes. Friendly little beast. Not very popular in this bar though."

"I should think not," said Miss Shapely. "Don't you ever *think* of bringing that savage brute here again."

"Wouldn't hurt a fly."

"That may or may not be true, but my bar's *not* a menagerie, Mr Raydell."

Miss Shapely moved away to honour someone by serving him.

Raydell laughed.

"She didn't take kindly to Angela," he said. "I had to come and make peace with her a few nights later. At first I didn't think she'd serve me, but, as you see, she relented. It was old Dan Westmacott who brought her round."

"*Dan* Westmacott?"

"Yes. Dante, his full name is. Neighbour of mine and a dam' good chap. Not like that sissified brother of his. We came in together."

"Which night would that have been?"

"The night those two poor women were murdered. In fact driving home I must have passed quite close to the body of one. Just near Goggs' cottage. Goggs works for me."

"Yes. You must have if you went that way home after ten."

"More like one in the morning. I had to meet someone after they shut."

"I see."

91

"You must allow us rustics our pleasures."

"I should be the last to want to interfere with them. What about Westmacott?"

"Oh, he went off somewhere soon after we'd conciliated Shapely."

"You didn't see him again?"

"Not that evening."

"And you arrived here at what time?"

"Couldn't have been long after opening time. When I eventually got in my old housekeeper was waiting for me. She's deaf as a post and gets very worried if anything unusual takes place. That evening she happened to be sitting near the telephone soon after we'd gone out when she heard it ring. She never hears it in the ordinary way. She picked up the receiver but couldn't get a word. She thinks it was a woman's voice. She imagined all sorts of things, poor old girl. Thought I'd driven into a ditch or dropped dead or something. When I was late coming home she nearly went out of her mind."

"Did you ever hear what the call was?"

"Never; I don't get many calls, either."

"You say you came in to town with Dante Westmacott. Do you mean you shared a car?"

"No. We both had things to do in the town. We came in each under his own steam, agreeing to meet here. You should come and meet Dan. Nice chap. His wife's our local beauty. When you've had enough of the old trouts at the Hydro come out to Lilbourne and feast your eyes on Gloria Westmacott. She's something."

"Thanks. Was either of you acquainted with Miss Carew?"

"I wasn't. I believe Dan had met her once. Anyway, why not come out for a drink tomorrow evening? I'll ask Dan and Gloria and you can have a good natter. You may find out something useful. Say about six?"

"Thanks. I'd like to."

"I'd be pleased to see this thing cleared up. Damnable business—two old ladies."

"Did you know Mrs Westmacott?"

"Not directly. But funnily enough my old housekeeper did. Years ago, it seems. She can tell you a good deal about her in her young days."

"What's your housekeeper's name?"

"Lightfoot. Grace Lightfoot. Most inappropriate because she clumps about like an elephant. Well, see you tomorrow."

Carolus watched him push his way to the other end of the bar, where he joined a large group.

"Wonder *why* he should be so keen on my going out there."

"Perhaps he wants you to see his ocelot."

"Perhaps. This place is getting packed, isn't it?"

"But not out of control. Shapely's got them where she wants them. Is there anyone else with whom you want to scrape acquaintance?"

"Yes. Three if we're lucky enough. Gilling the car-park man from the Granodeon. I gather he never misses. Two other possibles—Wright the chauffeur and Bickley who works for the Westmacotts."

"Don't expect too much."

"We'll see."

10

THE bar of the Dragon was now at its most crowded. It was a large room, but there was little empty floor space and the few tables and many chairs left almost no room in which customers could move about. There were not many women in the bar and the few there seemed to keep as far from Miss Shapely as possible.

"It doesn't do," she confided in Carolus. "It's all right if they come in with a gentleman, otherwise I don't encourage it. You never know."

"Quite," said Carolus understandingly.

Conversation was animated but never rowdy, and there were no groups of men who stood with bent heads while one of them talked in a low voice till all stood up to laugh— in other words no dirty stories. Miss Shapely dealt with demands for drinks or deputed them to Fred, and all was order and decorum.

"We've missed dinner," said Rupert Priggley. "Do you think we could get a sandwich?"

Carolus asked Miss Shapely.

"I'll send to the kitchen," she said, as though unable in her august situation to deal with the matter directly.

"Has Gilling come in yet?"

Was it possible that there was a faint suggestion of softening, of warmth almost, in Miss Shapely's manner? That could not possibly be a blush on her cheek, but did not her eyes sparkle a mite?

"Yes. That's Mr Gilling by the door. That very quiet respectable-looking gentleman with the raincoat."

The description made Mr Gilling unmistakable and Carolus soon had him in conversation. He was respectable to the point of despondency.

"You look after the cars at the Granodeon, don't you?"

"Only to Oblige, I do. I've got my pension from the army and don't need to do it. But I like to do something and the doctor told me I oughtn't to be idle. It's my kidneys."

"Yes?"

"Chronic. I get cold shivers, racking headaches, pains all down my back. Still, we have to carry on, don't we?

Can't give way. I look after the car-park, yes. But I was only saying to Miss Shapely the other day, I don't think I can keep on with it. Too much of a strain for anyone in my condition."

"But you were there on the night of the murders?"

"I'm there every night. It's the Worst Thing for me, I daresay, but we must do something. I wouldn't mind so much if it weren't for my gall-stones. Play me up properly, they do. Put the liver out of order. You don't know what they are till you've had them."

"Don't you get treatment?"

"Certainly I do. I don't know what we should do without the National Health."

"Well, we couldn't afford to have kidney *and* liver trouble."

"They're nothing to speak of really. We have to make the best of things, don't we?"

"Will you have a drink?"

"I'll have a little gin. I'd dearly like a nice light ale, but I daren't touch it. It's my flatulence. I get awful pains just here over the heart and palpitations you wouldn't believe. Then the giddiness. No, I daren't touch beer or tea. I'll just have a little gin to relieve it, because that's the best thing."

"Do you remember that evening, Mr Gilling?"

"I'm not likely to forget it. I had a terrible day that Thursday. It was my ulcer. Vomiting all day, I was. I thought to myself, I can never go on duty tonight with this. But there you are, we have to, don't we? Yes, I remember that Thursday."

"What time did you get to the car-park?"

"I nearly always get there round about four o'clock unless I'm suffering too much. Then at five I slip up to the café, where the manageress lets me have a cup of coffee. She's a friend of Miss Shapely's and a very nice respectable person. Then I stay in the car-park most of the time till nine o'clock, after which I come over here. You see, I can't walk about much. Lumbago."

"Lumbago?"

"Acute. All round the lower part of the back. I can hardly get up when I've once sat down, and as for walking anywhere—well, I couldn't do it. Yes, I was over at the car-park that day till nine."

"You don't remember Miss Carew's car being brought in?"

"No. It wasn't. Not while I was there. I knew her car well. She'd nearly always got the dog with her and used to leave it in the car when she went into the pictures. She'd sometimes leave me a few biscuits or a bone or something to give him if he got restless. I knew her, too. She never forgot to ask after my chilblains, because she'd suffered with them, too, and told me the best thing for them—painting with iodine. I should have noticed if she'd come in."

"Suppose someone else was driving her car?"

"I should have seen it. No, it must have come in after nine o'clock since they found it there in the morning. Between nine and half-past ten, about, when the entrance is locked."

"But if someone brought it in then wouldn't he or she have been taking a risk of being seen afterwards? Leaving the car-park, I mean?"

"No. There's a way out round the back for anyone on foot. Leads into Station Road. He could have put the car in and gone out that way."

"Or she could."

"Miss Carew, you mean? Wasn't she dead by then?"

"We don't know the time of her death."

Mr Gilling seemed taken aback by that.

"I thought you knew that," he said. "You mean she might have gone out to where she was found in someone else's car?"

"Why not? Do you know a farmer called Raydell?"

96

"Yes. Just left here, hasn't he? He upset Miss Shapely the other day."

"Do you know his car?"

"Yes, but I can't say whether it was in the park that night. It is sometimes, but I can't remember every car that comes in. I very often wait till they've parked them and give them their ticket as they go out. I can't run round with my sciatica. It cripples me in this weather. Have to Lay Up with it some days. You don't know what it is."

"So you can't really say what other cars were in the park that night?"

"No. I can't. Not to be sure. I remember Miss Carew's wasn't because I heard about her next day, and remembered at once. Otherwise I shouldn't. I forget things, you see. With these fits of neuralgia I get, things go out of your mind."

"You can't, for instance, recall whether Miss Tissot's chauffeur brought her car in?"

"We can very soon ask him because that's him over there. Just come in. Very respectable young man. Miss Shapely thinks a lot of him, I believe. Shall I call him across?"

"Yes," said Carolus.

"I shall have to go over and get him," explained Mr Gilling. "I can't make my voice heard with this laryngitis I get. Seems to come on worse in the evening."

But at that moment young Wright saw that Mr Gilling was attempting to catch his attention and came over.

"Evening, Mr Gilling," he said. "How are your varicose veins?"

"Terrible, yesterday, they were. Swelled up to twice the size. I thought I should have to go into hospital with them. But we mustn't give in, must we? Make the best of things. This gentleman wanted to know if your car was in my park on the night of the murders?"

Wright looked startled, as well he might at this question.

He was a tall very solemn-looking young man with something furtive and restless in his brown eyes.

"Are you Mr Deene, sir?" he asked Carolus. "Yes? Miss Tissot told me you were investigating. I hope I can give you some helpful information. Yes, the car was in the cinema car-park because Miss Tissot had given me permission to drive it that evening. I was taking my young lady to the pictures."

"Did you need the car for that?"

"My young lady lives about three miles out at a village called Tillshill, and I went to fetch her and afterwards drove her home."

"She would remember that?"

"Oh, I don't know. I shouldn't like her asked. She comes of very respectable people. Her father is the postmaster."

"That's all very well, Wright, but aren't you forgetting that two women have been murdered? If you need an alibi the 'respectability' of your girl's parents will have to be outraged. This is a serious matter."

"But why should I need an alibi, Mr Deene?"

"I don't know that you will. I said *if* you need an alibi. What time did you go to the pictures?"

"The half-past six house. Came out before nine."

"Then what did you do?"

"Went and had a coffee in the cinema tea-room."

"And after that?"

"I drove my young lady home."

"Straight home?"

"We had a little run round."

"In which direction?"

"Lilbourne way, if you want to know."

"That's in the opposite direction from Tillshill, isn't it?"

"Almost. Yes. It was just a little run round."

"I see. Did you come back through Buddington?"

"Yes, as a matter of fact we did."

"What time would that have been?"

"I don't know. We'd just had a little run round."

"About eleven?"

"Certainly not later."

"Then you drove out to Tillshill?"

"Yes. Straight away."

"No little run round this time?"

"No."

"So you were back at the hotel with the car parked before midnight?"

"Well before."

"Anyone see you?"

"I don't think so. There was no one at the hotel garage. All asleep. I met no one on my way to bed."

"How do you like working for Miss Tissot?"

"Miss Tissot is a Lady, Mr Deene. I owe everything to her, including my education. She had me taught to drive."

"Yet she was thinking of doing without a car, wasn't she?"

"Some of her investments were disappointing. She thought she might not be able to afford it. But of course now she has come into money from Miss Carew."

"So you will keep your job?"

"Oh I don't think Miss Tissot would have let me go in any case."

"Now please answer this carefully, Wright. On that Thursday on which the two old ladies were murdered did you see or hear or notice anything which you think might be important? Either in Buddington or on the Lilbourne road or anywhere else?"

Wright seemed to consider this.

"There was one small thing, but I don't like to mention it and I don't think it has anything to do with the murders."

Mr Gilling, who had remained with them, seemed the most interested member of Wright's small audience.

"Let's hear it, anyway," suggested Carolus.

"It was after the pictures. When I took my young lady for a little run round. We happened to stop for a moment . . ."

"Where was this?"

"Out on the Lilbourne road."

"But where exactly? Or don't you know?"

"From what I've heard since, I imagine it was very near where Miss Carew's body was found. It was just before you come to a cottage standing alone on the right hand side of the road."

"And what time would it have been?"

"I suppose it was getting on for eleven. We just happened to stop for a minute. We were sitting there talking when suddenly my young lady gave a kind of scream. There was a face at the window of the car."

"Could you see it clearly?"

"I should recognize it again. I suppose my eyes were used to the darkness . . ."

"I should think they were by that time."

"Anyway I saw a man with a big ginger moustache staring in."

"Never seen him before?"

"No. In a few moments I got out of the car, but it was too late. He was cycling away. I shouted, but he wouldn't stop. I went to pick up a stone to throw at him, because naturally I was very angry. As I did so I saw something white by the side of the road which I thought was a piece of paper. I don't know what made me pick it up. It was the flower of a lily, just the single bell."

"I see. You didn't try to follow this Peeping Tom in the car?"

"No. He was going away from Buddington and my young lady was very upset and wanted to get home."

"Of course she was," put in Mr Gilling sympathetically. "Any respectable young lady would have been. I shouldn't have liked it myself, suffering as I do from nerves. I go cold all over and can't hardly breathe. It's as though my heart was going to stop beating. I don't wonder your young lady felt it."

"That's all you have to tell me, Wright?"

"Yes, Mr Deene. I hope you won't say anything to Miss Tissot about this. She's very particular, as you know."

"She knows you have a girl?"

"She knows about my young lady, yes. I don't tell her more than that, because she's above such things, if you understand what I mean. She's a real lady, Miss Tissot is, and won't have anything to do with them in the hotel."

"I'm much obliged to you both for your information. Does either of you know Bickley by sight?"

"I know him," said Gilling, "but he's not here tonight. She never comes in. TT, I believe. He doesn't so often come in since Mrs Westmacott bought them a television set. I can't look at that myself because of my eyes. I get them sore and inflamed if I'm not careful and have to bathe them with boracic. But Mr and Mrs Bickley seem to like it and stay at home looking at it. He won't come in now because it's nearly closing time. Yes, I will have a little more gin and water, sir. It's the only thing I Dare Touch."

Wright had impatiently waited for a chance to address Carolus.

"What do you think about the murders, sir? Miss Tissot doesn't like to discuss them, but I believe her opinion is that they must have been the work of a maniac."

"Of course they were," said Mr Gilling. "What else could they have been? They were both respectable ladies."

"Do you think so, sir?" pressed Wright.

"No. I don't. Nor do the police, so far as I can judge." He turned to Priggley. "We must get our sandwiches," he said.

When Carolus and Rupert managed to escape to the

corner of the bar in which they had started the evening, Miss Shapely handed them their sandwiches rather as though she were presenting the prizes after the school sports. They ate these gratefully but in silence.

When they returned the empty plate to the bar Miss Shapely condescended to ask how they had got on.

"I saw you talking to Mr Carew," she said, "and afterwards to that Mr Johnson. I'm pleased to say they've both gone. I have to be careful when they're here because I know they're both given to using Language."

Carolus begged her to have a drink with him.

"It's not often I accept a drink," said Miss Shapely, "but I will have a touch of gin."

She poured out a measure of water from a bottle with the familiar Gordon's Gin label on it and beamed on them magnificently.

"And how did you get on with Mr Gilling?" she asked gently.

"Very well," said Carolus. "He gave me some first-rate information for my . . . programme."

"I'm sure he did. He's a most respectable gentleman is Mr Gilling. It's a shame he lost his wife some years ago."

"He seems to suffer from a number of ailments," said Carolus mildly.

"Poor man. It's living alone like that. Makes him dwell on things."

There was a pause during which Miss Shapely gave an unmistakable sigh and a glance in Gilling's direction.

"What he wants, what Mr Gilling wants, is Looking After," she said.

Her reverie seemed to end abruptly with the realization that it was nearly closing-time. She made no mention of this aloud, but whispered to Fred to 'shout time'.

Carolus told Rupert on the way home that he would have to see John Moore again soon.

"I suppose that means you're what you call 'getting somewhere'?"

"Distinctly. Yes."

"Know who did it?"

"Better than that. I know *why*."

11

"Two more lots to see," said Carolus, "then I think some action."

"Action?" yawned Rupert from the depths of an arm-chair in the Lounge of the Royal Hydro.

"Yes. This case isn't going to be cleared up by question and answer and a solution like a crossword's."

"But what do you mean by action? Crawling about with a magnifying glass?"

"If you were a human boy instead of a hybrid monstrosity you would have read your *Stalky and Co* and would remember Stalky's favourite quotation: 'the bleating of the kid excites the tiger'. You can think over that."

"I have," said Rupert promptly. "And it doesn't seem to promise much but corn. If you suppose that at your time of life you can turn yourself into one of these hard-boiled, steel-gutted, lynx-eyed American sleuths who carry guns and risk their lives every few pages, you're wildly mis-taken. You're English, sir, as English as Sherlock Holmes and Hercule (*Ma foi!*) Poirot. You'll never be one of Raymond Chandler's boys. *Stalky and Co!* That's just about your mark."

"Thank you, Priggley."

"I mean, hadn't you better grow up, sir? This is a

nasty business you're investigating. Really nasty. You talk about seeing two more lots of witnesses or suspects or what have you, then, you say, 'some action'. Meanwhile I suppose some other poor old girl will have had it."

"That," said Carolus firmly, "is what I am going to prevent. But not, as you rightly suggest, by walking about armed. It perhaps hasn't occurred to you that before catching your murderer it is as well to identify him. I have yet to have drinks at Mr Raydell's farm to meet his neighbours, Dante Westmacott and his wife."

"She's supposed to be beautiful or something, isn't she?"

"She is."

"Well, that's one lot. Who are the others?"

"The others are Mr Maurice Ebony and his assistant Moira."

"At least we shall have a day in town then."

"I shall have to go up, yes."

"Well, you know what you're doing. I don't deny that in your old-fashioned way you generally seem to narrow the thing down to someone with a reasonable amount of evidence against him."

A pageboy with a small tray handed Carolus a letter.

"Unless I'm mistaken," said Rupert, eyeing this; "that is the handwriting of your employer."

"It's from the headmaster," admitted Carolus, noting the Brighton postmark.

"Oh, come on, Sir. Show."

"Certainly not. Go and clean the car while I read it."

When he was alone he opened Mr Gorringer's letter, which was headed The Sandringham Private Hotel, Brighton.

My Dear Deene,

In conveying to you my best wishes and those of Mrs Gorringer for your speedy recovery, I feel bound to touch on two matters which have greatly concerned me. It has come to my ears that the boy Priggley, who had instructions from his father to place himself in the care of a private tutor for the duration of the holidays, has not, as I strongly advised, gone with the Hollingbournes to Cornwall, but has betaken himself to Buddington-on-the-Hill where you are recuperating.

The boy's father, I feel, is greatly to blame in allowing his precocious offspring to make his own arrangements in this way, but *entre nous* I have reason to know that Priggley *père* is not a man of high moral rectitude and in fact is spending his time in Italy, where he has formed a *liaison* of a most undesirable character. He has, however, allowed Priggley no less a sum than £20 a week to be paid to his temporary guardian, and this would have been a *godsend* to Hollingbourne with his growing family. I readily acquit you of any mercenary motive in the matter, my dear Deene, since I know too well that your ample private income enables you to be indifferent to things which for us labourers in the vineyard are important. But I hope you will perceive how unfortunate is the situation vis-à-vis Hollingbourne, who naturally feels that he has been deprived of one of the few plums our exacting profession has to offer.

The other matter is even graver. Unless my ears deceived me I heard before leaving Newminster a rumour that contrary to your doctor's orders and my expressed wishes you are again jeopardizing the fair name of the Queen's School by embroiling yourself in detective work of a nature likely to result in unfortunate publicity. Can this be true? Scarcely out of bed after an illness which deprived us of your help in the term's examinations, is it possible that you are so ill-advised as to dabble in things better left to the police? If it is indeed the case I feel I have no alternative but to cut short my holiday here and come with all speed to Buddington in order to salvage what I can of the school's reputation.

I do not wish to be hypocritical about this. It happens that the Sandringham Private Hotel has changed hands since our last stay here and the new proprietors show no disposition to study our comforts as their predecessors did. So I will not pretend that a shortening of my stay would be altogether unwelcome.

I still hope and trust that the rumour which reached me is false and that you are taking a thorough rest in preparation for next term. But I feel bound to ask for your reassurance on this point to make my plans accordingly.

Mrs Gorringer sends you her best wishes and wittily adds that she hopes you won't allow Priggley to be priggish.

> I remain, my dear Deene,
> Yours sincerely,
> HUGH GORRINGER.

To this Carolus wrote an immediate reply on the elaborately embossed notepaper of the Royal Hydro.

DEAR HEADMASTER,

Many thanks to you and Mrs Gorringer for your good wishes. I have quite recovered from jaundice and feel extremely fit.

If Hollingbourne can manage to persuade himself that the care of Priggley is 'a plum', as you say, I am sorry. I regard it as an unmitigated nuisance and did my best to send the little brute down to Cornwall. Nor do I think Hollingbourne would find there was much profit from the boy's allowance when his wine, cigarette and hotel bills have been paid. If it were not for Priggley's extraordinary luck or skill in backing horses I imagine he would show a loss.

As for the double murder, yes it's a most interesting case. I hope to get it cleared up before the beginning of term. If you would like to come here for the *dénouement* you will find this hotel comfortable in a nursing-home sort of way.

With kind regards to you both,

Yours sincerely,
CAROLUS DEENE.

Carolus decided that on his way out to Furlongs Farm, Raydell's place at Lilbourne, he would call at the lonely cottage and see Mrs Goggs. Something he had learned in the bar of the Dragon made her evidence on one point interesting. Priggley was against this.

"You keep saying that there was a powerful intellect behind this murder," he reminded Carolus. "What on earth can farm labourers and such have to do with it?"

"Even if homicidal tendencies did not often inspire the most stupid, there can be a planner and an executive in any crime. But that's beside the point in the particular enquiry I want to make."

It was dusk as he approached the cottage, and it certainly had a somewhat desolate look on that lonely road. Nor was the appearance of Mrs Goggs less wild than that of her home as the wind blew her dark hair over her face. There was something gypsyish about her, Carolus decided.

She showed no disposition to ask them into the house this time; indeed she made it clear at once that she was just giving her husband his tea and could not waste time or catch her death out here in this wind. Yet when she understood what had brought Carolus to visit her again she was ready enough to talk.

"Mrs Goggs, the other day you said that you were not on speaking terms with Thickett. Would you mind telling me the cause of that?"

"I don't know whether it's anyone's business only mine," she said, "but if you knew what I know you'd feel the same."

"Yes?"

"No excuse for it either. With two girls grown up and

one married. You'd have thought anyone would be ashamed."

"Of what?"

"I said to my husband, if I was ever to catch *him* up to such larks I don't know what I wouldn't do. But Goggs has more respect."

"Than?"

"I can't understand it myself. A man with a wife and children. I wonder the police have never done anything about it."

"What?"

"I don't say a lot of them oughtn't to be ashamed of themselves, but coming all this way on his bicycle at night. It's not right, is it?"

"You haven't quite explained."

"Peeping and prying, that's what. Cycling up to cars and seeing what there is to see through the window, then cycling off. It's not very nice, is it?"

"No," admitted Carolus.

"Cunning, too. Always off the way the car's turned away from so that no one would catch him. You ask my husband. I must run in now. If that isn't reason enough I don't know what is."

"Thank you, Mrs Goggs."

A malicious leer came into her face.

"Why? You don't think he's done it, do you?"

"I've no opinions yet."

"It wouldn't surprise me," said Mrs Goggs. "I wouldn't put anything past him."

She turned round abruptly and without saying good night disappeared round the corner of the house. Carolus drove on to Lilbourne.

Raydell himself came to the door of his old farmhouse and led Carolus and Priggley into a pleasant room with a low ceiling. A log fire burned in a huge open fireplace and the atmosphere was cheerful. "I've not asked the Westmacotts until seven," said Raydell, "because I thought you ought to meet my old housekeeper. She knew Dante's mother as a girl."

"I should like to," said Carolus.

"Don't try to talk to her. She can just hear me because she's used to my voice, but she won't know what you want. She doesn't need much encouragement to talk about the past."

She didn't. She was a lumbering old creature with a wizened sallow face and she began to talk as if by clockwork. Carolus had the impression that she had gone over her rather dim memories very often before this to inquisitive listeners.

"They all died together," she began equivocally. Carolus listened with interest but she at once explained herself. "Well, all within seven years of one another. Madox Brown was the first to go in 1893, then Christina Rossetti the next year, William Morris and Millais in '96, Burne-Jones two years later and Ruskin in 1900. I always said there was something funny about it."

"Ask her about Mrs Westmacott," said Carolus, whose taste for irrelevance was not without limits.

Raydell did.

"I was a sort of companion to her," said Miss Lightfoot. "She being a model."

On this interesting and suggestive statement she did not enlarge.

"Supposed to be beautiful, she was. Just right for pictures of the saints. She wouldn't have done for it lately, would she? Though you couldn't tell her that. She still thought she ought to be in a stained glass window. Nearly eighty and expected to look like someone with a halo on. It made me laugh, really, only not to her face. I'm not saying she wasn't kind, but the bit of money she's left me has come too late. _I_ don't think I ought to be done in oils. I'm satisfied to stay where I am."

Carolus nodded encouragement.

"Mind you, she was lucky, was Rosie Betts. Yes, that was her name, but professionally she was known as Rosamond. She came from the same part of London as I did, but there was no doubt about it, she was very much sought after. They all had a go at her. You can see her in their paintings to this day. Then she met this Westmacott. He had all the money in the world, left him by his father who'd died with all the rest of them, in '95 as a matter of fact. He was about the same age as she was.

"I didn't see her for years after that, though she used to write to me sometimes. But it was through her I came here to look after Mr Raydell after his wife was killed in an air raid in London. I went to see her now and again, but she wouldn't go about much and used to be taken to church in a bathchair, though she could walk around the house as well as you or I."

"When did they meet last?" Carolus asked Raydell.

"Not for a month or more," said Miss Lightfoot when this had been put to her. "I'm not as active myself as I was and she was very taken up with her church and that. I'm Wesleyan and have no patience with all that bowing and scraping she went in for."

There was the sound of a bell and Raydell, saying it was the Westmacotts, stood up. Miss Lightfoot remarked without much enthusiasm that she hoped Carolus would find out who had murdered her old friend, and left them, clumping heavily from the room.

It occurred to Carolus when he met Dante Westmacott and his wife that none of those connected with the two old murdered ladies had shown much disposition to mourn them. He realized that in England the wearing of black clothes and strict rules of mourning had gone out when the first world war brought the necessity for mourning to most homes and the thing had lapsed through excess. He did not expect to see widows' weeds and crêpe arm-bands, but surely near relatives, in this case a son and daughter-in-law, might have been a little less jovial in manner and flamboyant in dress.

Dan Westmacott was a big jolly man in a glaring check suit with a brass-buttoned vermilion waistcoat and a loud tie. His wife was, Carolus agreed with general opinion, a very beautiful woman, and her mustard-coloured tweeds set off the brilliance of her own colouring.

Raydell was soon shaking cocktails, and chatter and the smell of dry Martinis filled the air.

"How is Angela?" Dan asked Raydell.

"She is in splendid form but I haven't taken her to the Dragon again. You shall see her presently, Deene. She's an endearing creature."

"Is Angela your ocelot? I'd like to see her."

"I'm on Miss Shapely's side," said Gloria Westmacott musically. "Angela is not the creature to take into a crowded bar."

Dan turned to Carolus.

"I've read of some of your cases," he said. "I hope you get to the bottom of this one. My mother and I did not see eye to eye about a good many things. My brother was her favourite. But it's damned distressing to know that she was strangled. Yes, I will have another, Ray."

"Did you know the other victim?" asked Carolus abruptly and with such point that the question could not be ignored. It caused rather an awkward pause and Dan looked at his wife.

"Yes, as a matter of fact I did. Met her through the people she lived with."

"The Baxeters."

"Don't ask me how I came to know them first, because I can't remember. But for a long time now, must be a couple of years, they've been driving out to my farm to buy what they call fresh produce, because it seems that anything which has gone through the hands of a retailer is contaminated so far as they're concerned. They're cranks, as you know."

"You met Miss Carew at their house?"

Dan smiled to Raydell.

"I didn't know I was going to be put through a catechism when I met Deene," he said good-humouredly. "But of course I don't mind telling you anything you want to know. I met her there at lunch. Extraordinary occasion. Thank God they had provided a couple of chops for Sophia Carew and me, because the rest of it was inedible. Radish and aubergine soup, forcemeat rissoles, lentil fritters, hominy croquettes, that sort of thing. I liked old Sophia, though. Game old girl, I thought. I was damned sorry to hear about her death."

"May I ask you one more question, Mr Westmacott? On the evening of the two murders you left Raydell early after conciliating Miss Shapely. Where did you go?"

Dante Westmacott flushed with annoyance.

"This is going too far," he said. "You are asking me to produce an alibi. Are you going to suggest I murdered my own mother?"

"I'm not suggesting anything. But you're one of the people most closely connected with the case and it is as well for everyone's sake, if I'm going to clear this thing up, that I should know where you were when the two women were killed."

"He's quite right, dear," said Gloria unexpectedly.

"But it's ridiculous. I don't see why I should discuss the thing. Have you asked my brother this?"

"Yes. He has given me an account of his movements that evening."

"I see. I have nothing to hide, but I resent being asked. However, after leaving Raydell I drove out here to pick up Gloria in time to take her to the pictures. Last house at the Granodeon."

"Did you see Gilling the car-park attendant?"

"Of course I saw Gilling," said Dante Westmacott, whose joviality seemed to have given place to irritation.

"He was telling us about his eczema, remember, dear?" said Gloria.

"Something of the sort. What more do you want to know?"

"After the pictures . . ."

"After the pictures we came straight home."

"By the usual route? That is to say, past the quarry?"

"Naturally. There's no other way out here, unless you make an enormous detour."

"You haven't any idea about these murders, Mr Westmacott? You knew of no one, for instance, who had threatened your mother or anything of the sort?"

"No. So far as I know my mother was popular in the town. She ought to have been, anyway. She gave enough money away."

"You have no suspicions?"

"None that I want to repeat. I gather that the police think the murders were done by someone at least temporarily insane. Don't you share that view?"

"Not if by insane you mean someone with a mania for homicide. No, I think there was another motive."

"How could there be? There was no connection between the women. Who could have a motive for killing both?"

"There were certain links," said Carolus quietly.

At that moment Raydell, who had left the room a few minutes earlier, returned with the ocelot. She was a handsome creature, not much larger than a large domestic cat, and seemed perfectly restful and at home. Her smooth yellowish fur was beautifully spangled with black rings above, and her chest was white.

Everyone, glad it seemed of the diversion, made a fuss of her.

12

CAROLUS had made an appointment by telephone with Maurice Ebony and set out for London next morning to keep it.

The All-British Bullion Company, it seemed, had its offices in Mersey Street off the Tottenham Court Road. Had Carolus imagined these to be as palatial as the name was resounding he would have been disappointed, for Mersey Street was mean and murky, running into a region of small Cypriot restaurants and foreign newsagents.

He found the building, but its ground floor was occupied by a barber's shop and the staircase behind an open door looked dirty and forbidding. He asked in the shop where he might find Mr Ebony and was told on the first floor. Climbing, he knocked at the nearest door, which was opened at once by a pleasant-looking girl.

"Come in," she said. "Maurice will be through in a minute. He's just shaving."

Carolus entered a tawdry sitting-room and sat there to wait.

Ebony, when he entered, was a surprise, a smooth and impeccable man in his thirties, glossy from his slick dark hair and brown moustache to his brilliant patent-leather shoes. He wore pin-stripe trousers and a blackcoat. He was civil enough to Carolus but seemed alert, if not a little nervous.

"You wanted to see me?"

"Yes, Mr Ebony. I'm investigating the double murder at Buddington."

"What's it to do with me?"

"You're the missing link," said Carolus evenly. "You're one of the very few people who had dealings with both the murdered women."

"Look, Mr Deene, my business is gold-buying, nothing else. I don't know anything about the murders."

"No? We don't always know how much we *do* know, Mr Ebony. Would you mind telling me about your experiences in Buddington?"

"I went down there to buy gold."

"Of course. I imagine it was a good place for that?"

"It was once. There've been too many nibbling at it. In this job the competition's fierce."

"Still a town of elderly retired people . . ."

"They've been milked dry, Mr Deene. Scarcely a scrap of red left in the place. My assistant had a job to find me an In at all."

"The first was the Baxeters', perhaps?"

"That the Colonel and his wife? I remember. They may live on potato peelings and porridge, but d'you know what they did? Produced their own set of scales. Would you believe it?"

"You didn't mind that, of course?"

"N-no. But it seemed a liberty. Their own scales. I only bought a couple of scraps. Then this Miss Carew came in and I was able to buy a few bits and pieces. At market prices, of course."

"What about that gold chain of hers?"

"Silver gilt," said Mr Ebony.

Carolus suddenly leaned across and pulled forward the lapel of the other's immaculate black jacket. Behind it was some white paste.

"Silver gilt, Mr Ebony? Then why do you keep silver nitrate paste behind your lapel?"

"Smart, aren't you? Who put you up to this lark?"

"I'm not a man of action, Mr Ebony. I'm a schoolmaster. I believe in books. But when I found myself caught out as an ignoramus in the art of gold-clapping I looked it up."

"Where?"

"In a book called *Smiling Damned Villain* by Rupert Croft-

Cooke. It is the life-story of a criminal called Paul Axel Lund, among whose other activities was a spell of gold-clapping. He gives very explicit details."

"The lousy grass."

"They enabled me to understand how your 'silver gilt' chain from Miss Carew was bought. How long did it take?"

"I was only with her about half an hour."

"Then you saw Mrs Westmacott and had what you described as a gobble."

"I bought some stuff, yes. But there was no silver gilt about that. In fact I left a deposit on some gold which I haven't been back to collect."

"The Swotch, eh?"

"What do you mean the Swotch? You've been reading too much detective fiction."

"This wasn't fiction. It was fact."

"We've all got a living to earn."

"Very true. Did you buy from anyone else?"

"No. I never had another touch."

"Have you been down to Buddington again?"

"Yes. As a matter of fact I came through there yesterday. That will show you I've nothing to be afraid of in Buddington."

"Yesterday? Did you buy anything?"

"Look, Mr Deene, my business is legal. If I wanted to leave a deposit with Mrs Westmacott and not go back that's my business. I don't see that what I buy or who I buy from is anything to do with you."

Carolus stood up. He spoke very seriously.

"I'm not interested in your business *qua* business. I'm not a policeman. Your little frauds are no affair of mine, Mr Ebony. This is a matter of murder. Two harmless old women have been strangled and others may be in danger."

"But what's that to do with me?"

"Will you please believe me when I say that, whether

or not you're aware of it, it has a great deal? If you bought any gold yesterday from any woman in Buddington she may be in serious danger."

Maurice Ebony looked at Carolus fixedly.

"I don't want to bring trouble to anyone," he said. "At the same time I don't want trouble myself. I've seen too much of it."

"Where did you buy gold yesterday?"

"As a matter of fact it was from the woman who worked for Mrs Westmacott. Bickley, her name is. She knew about my buying the old lady's and asked me to come and see hers. There's proof that I give good prices and no funny business. She asked me at the time, only I waited till these murders had died down a bit. I bought from no one but her."

"What did you buy?"

"Nothing much. Old bits and pieces. They were the woman's own stuff, I'm sure. She told me about them while Mrs Westmacott was still alive."

"Did you talk about this while you were down there?"

"Certainly not. I never discuss my business with anyone. Least of all in a town like Buddington, where everyone knows everyone else's business."

"Who was present when you bought the gold?"

"Only the woman herself and just as we were talking business her husband came in."

"It was in their cottage?"

"Yes. But she took me over there. I called at the house, Rossetti Lodge."

"Leaving your car outside?"

"Yes."

"I daresay you've got a showy car of some kind, Mr Ebony?"

"Well yes. It's a Chev. You need a smart-looking car in my business. Gives confidence."

"Also left outside a house," said Carolus anxiously, "it

gives to anyone curious enough to enquire the information that the householder is selling gold to you. As the two old women did a few days before they were murdered."

"You know very well that must have been a coincidence."

"It is possible. But that doesn't change its significance now."

"I don't understand you, Mr Deene. I just mind my own business. I don't want anything to do with murders. Mine's a nice quiet little business."

"So is murder, Mr Ebony. Good-day."

Carolus was a good driver and ran out of London as fast as safety permitted. He did not speak and Priggley seemed a little impressed by his grim silence.

"Did you really mean that, about danger?" he asked.

"I did."

"You think the man who killed Sophia Carew and old Mrs Westmacott will, as they say, strike again?"

"I am fairly sure that there will be an attempt on the life of Mrs Bickley."

"But why, for heaven's sake? You say he's not a maniac?"

"I have told a number of people connected with the case that I don't think the murders were the work of a maniac. I have also let it be thought that the police don't."

"What are you going to do now?"

"Get back to Buddington as quickly as possible," said Carolus, accelerating on a piece of open road.

"And there?"

"See Inspector John Moore."

But John Moore was not encouraging.

"I know you have ingenious ideas, Carolus, but this time you seem to be stretching it. You ask me to believe that because Mrs Bickley sold some old gold to Ebony someone is going to try to strangle her."

"I said it was possible."

"But you don't tell me why."

"Can't you be satisfied with the fact that both the other women were killed after selling gold to this man?"

"Don't be absurd, Carolus."

"You told me it was the only link connecting the two households."

"Wasn't it?"

"No. In a small town like this you couldn't possibly have such mutually exclusive divisions. I can tell you several ways in which there was confusion. Dante Westmacott is a friend of a farmer called Raydell who is an acquaintance of Charles Carew. Raydell's housekeeper knew Mrs Westmacott before she was married and is a beneficiary in her will. Dante Westmacott was well acquainted with the Baxeters and had met Sophia Carew in their house. See what I mean?"

"Yes. But it only weakens your case about Ebony."

"Perhaps. But I am quite serious, John, in asking you to take precautions for Mrs Bickley."

"I should have to know a great deal more than you tell me."

"Are you making progress, John?"

"I have to admit we're not. A small point I forgot to tell you is that the upholstery of Sophia Carew's car has been badly ripped. But there's nothing concrete to go on. The case remains mysterious because of the two murders. As I told you right at the beginning I believe I could solve either one, but two are baffling. They make one introduce the most fantastic theories. A young assistant of mine calculates that on the facts we have there are no less than six possible lines of solution, discounting such complications as suspects. He puts them down like this, though not in order of probability:

1. A maniac whose aberration is homicidal, who has an obsession with elderly women.
2. A murderer who had motives, unknown to us, for both murders.

3. Two separate murderers working independently, one of whom, by a freak of chance, saw the first murder and made the second look like it.
4. Two murderers working independently, and an outsider who made their murders appear to resemble one another, in other words who adorned both corpses with lilies.
5. Two murderers working in collaboration, who agreed to make their crimes look alike.
6. The two women murdered together at Rossetti Lodge at the same time, the apparent difference in time accounted for by the fact that Mrs Westmacott's body remained in a warm room while Miss Carew's was left in the open.' "

"I could add several more to those," said Carolus gravely.

"It's quite preposterous. Those are only basic possibilities. When it comes to suspects, about the only thing we know is that the murderer of Miss Carew probably didn't wear size eight shoes."

"Have you checked on shoe sizes?"

"Yes, for almost every man even remotely connected with the case. Want to know them?"

"Please."

"There are none size seven. Size eights are worn by Ebony, Charles Carew, Colonel Baxeter and Gabriel Westmacott. Size nines Raydell, Gilling, Wright, Bickley, Ben Johnson. Size ten Dante Westmacott and Thickett. Helpful, isn't it?"

"Yes."

"As a matter of fact those shoes which were found, if they indicate anything at all, seem to me to suggest a woman as the murderer of Miss Carew. There's nothing physically impossible about that."

"Not if it was a woman of Mrs Baxeter's size and strength."

"Didn't need to be. Any woman of normal physique under, say, fifty could have done it. What else have we got? Two lilies stolen from a front garden in Station Road on the night of the murders and a lily found on each corpse. What's the good of that?"

"I should have thought a great deal—if you knew who stole the lilies."

"I don't," snapped Moore. "It could have been anyone in the town. Then there's another of these blasted dogs that barked in the night. That's all. Nothing to get your teeth into. While so far as times and alibis are concerned it seems possible for almost anyone in Buddington to have done both murders."

"Personally I looked for motive," said Carolus mildly.

"Oh, you did? And that's what brings you to think that we ought to protect Mrs Bickley?"

"Indirectly, yes."

"You're crazy, Carolus. You're a dabbler looking for complicated, intricate motives and mental processes, whereas I'm pretty sure that the truth here is a simple one."

"It is."

"Do you suggest by that cryptic remark that you know who killed these women?"

"Oh no," said Carolus, rather shocked. "Oh no, my dear John. If I knew that, I should tell you at once."

"Then what do you know?"

"Not who but why. I understand, I think, why both those women were killed that night. That has always seemed to me the important thing in this case. As for who did it, he, she or they will reveal himself . . ."

"Or herself, or themselves," put in Moore bitterly.

"Very soon now, I think," continued Carolus, unperturbed. "My only anxiety is lest the revelation costs another life. I wish you would protect Mrs Bickley, John."

"Do you know her?"

"Not yet. Nor her husband."

"They're not exactly the sort of people one would normally feel much alarm about. Bickley's an ex-policeman."

"No! Perhaps the revelation may come through someone else entirely. Heaven knows there are enough elderly women in the town."

"And it must be an elderly woman?"

"If I am right in my notions, yes."

"Then you *must* be thinking of a maniac, Carolus. I've thought that from the first. What we want here is a psychiatrist and I've a damned good mind to see if we can get one sent down, not to examine any particular suspect, because I haven't one, but to observe everybody in the case. Someone who appears reasonably normal, sane enough anyway to deceive those about him that he has no secret madness, must be going about . . ."

"Unless it really was a madman, John. An old-fashioned, out-and-out lunatic who has escaped from restraint."

"Don't pull my leg, Carolus. This case isn't a joke."

"No. And that reminds me, have you noticed anyone behaving as though he was sorry about the two old women? Anyone showing the slightest disposition to mourn them, for example?"

"I can't say I have."

"Nor I. And I find that odd. Distinctly odd. Oh well, I shall have to do what I can myself for Mrs Bickley."

"I believe that's a leg-pull, too."

"No, John, it's not," said Carolus gravely. "I only wish it were."

13

Mrs Bickley opened the door of Rossetti Lodge and invited Carolus to enter. She was small, neat and businesslike. As soon as she began to talk Carolus felt that here at last was someone who did not show indifference to the tragedy of recent events. She alone of all the friends and relatives of the two dead women seemed to be saddened by the loss of one of them.

"I was told to expect you, sir," she said to Carolus. "You are going to find out who did this dreadful thing, aren't you? If there's anything I or my husband can do we shall be pleased."

"Thank you, Mrs Bickley. I wonder who told you I would be coming to see you?"

"That was Mr Gabriel. He said you were sure to want to see where it happened."

"Yes. I should like to do that. And there are a good many questions I want to ask you, Mrs Bickley."

They were standing in the entrance hall of the house, furnished with William Morris mediaevalism. The wall-paper was of the original Morris printing of the Acanthus pattern of 1862 and the furniture, hangings, tiles and odd-ments of decoration had the unmistakable look of articles from the Pre-Raphaelite workshops. Mrs Bickley led the way to a small sitting-room leading off the hall, and here the pomegranate pattern glared from the walls and the shelves were full of books in Kelmscott editions. Two pieces of furniture contrasted with this, a long divan and in front of it a full-length mirror.

"This is where I found poor Mrs Westmacott," said Mrs Bickley in a subdued but steady voice. "She was lying on that couch full length and would have looked peaceful if it wasn't for her expression. That was awful, sir, and it

123

worries me to think that the last I saw of her was like that with her eyes popping out. You see, she was a very even-tempered old lady and in all the years we had been with her I'd never known her in a passion about anything. Yet that's what she looked in death, as though she had died in a fit of temper."

"The head was here?"

"On that cushion, yes, sir. She thought the world of those cushions. I don't understand a lot about it, but they were from someone's workshop and had been bought by Mr Westmacott's father; that's the old lady's father-in-law I mean, sir. Her head was there and her hands were folded round this lily stalk we've heard so much about. It's my belief she died on that sofa, because unless there was more than one of them she couldn't have been lifted there. She was very heavy, as you may know, and took more than anyone's strength to lift."

"There was no sign of a struggle?"

"Nothing at all, sir. The police went over everything for fingerprints and looked here, there and everywhere, but it was just as if no one had been here that night. If the doctor hadn't been sure she was strangled you'd have sworn she died natural."

"Did you know that Gabriel Westmacott came to see his mother that evening?"

"Oh yes, sir. He popped across to see us as he always does when he comes to the house. Mind you, he didn't stay long. Well, I like looking at the television same as anyone else, though there are times when my husband wants to throw something at it. That night it was so silly he said he wouldn't stand another minute and went round to the Dragon."

"What time would that have been?"

"Oh, quite early on. Long before Mr Gabriel came over. I was alone then. It can't have been more than eight when Bickley went. He didn't come back till after closing. Must have been half-past ten when he got in. But I was here the whole while, and if Mrs Westmacott had wanted anything she only had to ring. She had a private telephone line across to our place. But she never did."

"You don't know how long Gabriel Westmacott was with her?"

"I don't."

"Nor why he came?"

"Well, sir . . . I don't like to say anything . . ."

"He told me he had come because he needed some money and that Mrs Westmacott gave it to him."

"I'm afraid I don't quite believe that, sir. We had had this before."

"Really?"

"Mrs Westmacott had to hide her money, you see. It's not nice to talk about it, but I'm sure you won't make trouble. She liked to keep a large sum in the house and next morning I found it had gone. I haven't said anything to the police."

"I see. Now Mrs Westmacott is believed not to have been killed till midnight or thereabouts."

"We'd gone to bed by then, or rather I had. My husband sits up for a bit after he comes in at night with his evening paper. He's interested in horses. But he always puts the light out and doesn't wake me up. He would have heard if Mrs Westmacott had rung, up to half-past twelve, anyway."

"Who had a latch key of the house?"

"Only Mrs Westmacott and Mr Gabriel. And Mr Dan has still got his. We had our key of the back door, because we always came in and out that way."

"You are sure Dante Westmacott had one?"

"Mr Dan didn't very often come to the house, but when he did he always walked straight in."

"So you think someone must have been admitted by Mrs Westmacott herself? Someone she knew?"

125

"That's what it looks like. She wasn't at all the nervous sort and would go to the front door herself if she was up. If it had been very late and she wasn't expecting anyone, I daresay she would have rung over to us. But not if she knew who it was."

"She could move about quite easily?"

"In the house, she could. But she didn't like going out except in a bathchair. To tell you the truth, sir, I believe it would have done her good to have walked round as far as the church on Sundays, but there you are. As for going to the door, she would have thought nothing of it and always went up to bed on her own."

"At what time did you see her last, Mrs Bickley?"

"I always went across at nine. She didn't eat much at night, just a light meal about seven which I would get for her and take the tray away. She wasn't a lady to want fussing over or to put others out. I would come across at nine, put her hot-water bottle in her bed if it was at all chilly, then go down to see if there was anything she wanted. Sometimes she would keep me chatting for a while, then she would remember I liked the television and tell me to go and turn it on, as though it was a little joke of hers. That night she was reading. She didn't say anything about expecting Mr Gabriel, but just said good night at once and I left her. Never thinking, of course."

"Neither you nor your husband heard or saw anything unusual during the night?"

"No, sir. It was just like any other night, so far as we were concerned."

"And in the morning?"

"I don't generally come across here till just before nine. Mrs Westmacott didn't like being disturbed and the women who came in to clean never got here before then. When I came across that morning I put the kettle on in the kitchen to make Mrs Westmacott her tea, then came to this room to pull the curtains back. The door was shut as usual and I switched on the light to see my way across to the windows. I saw her at once lying there and thought I was going to faint. I knew she was dead . . ."

"How?"

"Well, lying there in the morning. Besides you should have seen her face. Oh, you couldn't doubt of it, but when I felt well enough I went and just touched her. She was as cold as ice."

"What did you do then?"

"Ran for my husband as quick as ever I could. He said afterwards I was white as a sheet and couldn't speak plainly. But when he realized what it was he went across, and as soon as he saw her and what she looked like he rang the police."

"Before calling a doctor?"

"He could see it wasn't any good doing that."

"Still . . ."

"Anyhow that's what my husband did, and it was a good thing, because the police brought their own doctor and we didn't have to have two. They very soon knew it was murder and of course that started everything. It was days before they'd let me do the room."

"What's this about a piece of wire with spangles in it?"

"More like stars, they were, like you have on a Christmas tree. They found that on that little table there behind her couch. I never noticed it when I came in—well, I was so upset by seeing poor Mrs Westmacott like that—but as soon as they found it they showed it to me and asked if I'd ever seen it before. I never had and told them so. Mrs Westmacott did not make much of Christmas as we know it, you see; she used to say Christmas cards and Christmas trees and that were all German nonsense, brought over by Prince Albert and written up by Dickens. When the two young gentlemen were at home she used to have a boar's head cooked and wouldn't look at a nice bit of turkey. It was all apiece with the furniture, which she said ought to go back to the Middle Ages. As for decorations like that, sparklers, and paper hangings, she wouldn't hear of them. So I knew those things must have been brought to the house, though what they were doing there I couldn't imagine."

"I see. Now tell me about this man who bought some old gold from Mrs Westmacott."

"Well, it was the young lady who came first. Ever so nice, she was, and explained about this Mr Ebony paying high prices. We never encourage anyone like that and always used to have *No Hawkers, No Canvassers, No Circulars* on the gate. But this young lady had a way with her and I said I'd just speak to Mrs Westmacott, in case. She had quite a lot of old gold stuff, from her family more than her husband's. So she agreed to see Mr Ebony when he came and they got on very well. When he started saying what he would give for the different pieces we were both surprised. Five pounds for this, six for that; well it came to about fifty pounds for what he said were the best pieces. The rest he just collected in a pile and said they were for the melting-pot and he could allow five pounds for the lot. When it came to paying he found he hadn't got enough money for the fifty pound lot, so he left a deposit of three pound on that. He just had enough to buy the little lot of rubbish for five pound and off he went. He never has taken the big lot."

"And never will," said Carolus. "Don't you see the swindle? The pieces he called rubbish were the only ones worth anything. He could afford to offer big prices for the others because he never intended to buy them. What, in fact, he did was to buy for eight pound about fifty pound worth of gold. Or more."

"I should never have thought it, sir. He seemed a very nice man. I told him at the time I had a few pieces and the day before yesterday he came and bought them. Very good prices he gave me, particularly as some of them turned out to be pinchbeck."

Carolus sighed.

"What time did he come?"

"In the afternoon."

"Do you know if he bought any more gold in Budding-ton?"

"I don't think so. He was on his way back from the coast and just called in before driving off to London."

"Was your husband there?"

"Oh yes, sir. But he never interferes with my business nor I with his. He was quite surprised at how much this Mr Ebony gave, in fact he said he wished he had some old gold to turn in, but he hadn't any. He'll be in presently and will tell you about it."

"Did you happen to mention it to Gabriel Westma-cott?"

"Yes, I did. I told him this Mr Ebony had been and not had enough money on him to take the other lot belonging to Mrs Westmacott, but that I'd sold him a few things of my own."

"Did you tell anyone else?"

"Well, the lady living opposite is a friend of mine. Mrs Plummer, that is, who looks after the big house you can see from here. I told her, because she's a person who thinks everything she does is clever and no one else knows anything."

Carolus smiled.

"Yes, I know Mrs Plummer. Anyone else?"

"I did happen to mention it to old Miss Lightfoot when I met her in the street yesterday. She's housekeeper to Mr Raydell out at Lilbourne and used to come and see Mrs Westmacott sometimes, so I knew her quite well. I could see she was looking at my purse when we were in a shop together and I didn't want her to Think Anything, so I told her where it came from. But I haven't mentioned to another soul."

At this point her husband appeared, a large grey-haired

ex-policeman who looked the part, and Carolus was introduced with explanations. Bickley, like his wife, appeared to have felt the loss of his employer.

"I don't know why you want to stay in this room," he said. "I don't like coming into it."

"The gentleman is asking about that man who bought the gold. He wants to know who knows about it?"

"Why? There's no secret. It was all your own stuff."

"It's not that," said Carolus. "I'll explain in a moment. But can you remember mentioning it to anyone?"

"Certainly I can. I had nothing to hide. I told them in the Dragon that night. It was as good as winning on a horse."

"Can you remember who was there, Mr Bickley?"

"Let's see. It was Miss Shapely I first mentioned it to and of course that Gilling was hanging round her, as he always is. But what surprised me was that Colonel Baxeter was in that evening, drinking lemon juice and asking to have the windows open, which Miss Shapely wouldn't hear of. He doesn't often come in, but he was there the night before last and heard what I said, because he told me his wife had sold some pieces to the same man. He said someone had told him that he'd been done over it, but he didn't believe it."

"Did you mention again that evening that Mrs Bickley had sold some gold to Ebony?"

"I daresay I did, because it was talked about in the bar."

"Who was there, Mr Bickley?"

"So far as I can remember much the usual crowd. One or two strangers I didn't know, but mostly regulars. Humpling the bootmaker. He's not often in. Charlie Carew. Young Wright the chauffeur. Mr Sawyer. Mr Dan was there and bought me a pint as he always does. That artist chap Johnson who I don't care for."

"Do you know a man called Thickett?"

"No. I can't say I do."

"You'd know if he came often to the Dragon?"

"Yes. I expect I should. But what is all this about, Mr Deene?"

"I don't want to sound alarming," said Carolus. "But I have reason to think that there may be another attempt at a murder."

"Oh dear," said Mrs Bickley. "Who is it going to be this time?"

Carolus looked uncomfortable.

"You see, both the two old ladies who were murdered had sold gold to Ebony . . ."

Bickley stood up.

"D'you mean he did it? That gold-buying chap?"

"Not necessarily. The point is that almost the only thing the two murdered women had in common was that they had purchased from Ebony. Now if there is to be another attempt . . ."

"You mean that he may try to attack my wife?" said Bickley.

"I hope I'm quite mistaken. But even if it was only a coincidence I think you ought to be careful. I don't think you ought to leave Mrs Bickley alone in the evening. It may be a false alarm, I may be as wrong as the police think I am, but all the same I think it's my duty to tell you. You've been in the police force, Mr Bickley. You will know what precautions to take."

Bickley stared at Carolus.

"If you'll forgive me saying so, I think what you say is out of all reason. Just because she sold a few pieces of gold to the same man . . ."

"You may be right. Still I'm sure you don't want to take any chances. I hope it will only be a short while before we have the man."

"Even if there's any truth in this, there must be others who sold stuff."

"Not that we know of, surely?"

"What about Mrs Baxeter?"

"Oh yes. I will see them. Of course, it was before the other murders that she sold it. Still, I'll make a point of seeing them. Thanks for reminding me."

"It's very upsetting," said Bickley.

"Not to me," said his wife. "I'm not afraid while Harry's with me, and it might be the means of finding out who did for poor Mrs Westmacott. Besides, I should be ready for him."

"Suppose there are several of them?"

"I don't think there will be anything you can't deal with, Bickley. Stranglers of women are not usually very heroic characters. I shan't worry so long as you take my warning seriously."

"Can't do anything else, can I?" said Bickley in a disgruntled way. "Why don't the police do something?"

"Because they think the idea is silly," said Carolus. "They're experienced men and may well be right. But I don't quite see how you can chance it."

"Nor do I. But it means I miss my pint at the Dragon, and ten to one it's all unnecessary."

"You'll have your television," Carolus pointed out.

Bickley's reply was unprintable.

14

FINDING that the Baxeters were not at home when he phoned, Carolus left a message asking them to get in touch with him as soon as possible. While he was awaiting this he was informed by the young woman at the reception desk that a Mr Gorringer had called and was expected to return at any moment.

All too soon Carolus found himself facing the headmaster. He wore a solemn and anxious expression.

"Well, Deene," he said, "this is a sorry state of things. The boy Priggley informs me that not only have you failed to elucidate the problem of the two murders but that you are actually expecting another."

"Priggley exaggerates," said Carolus. "I think it's possible that there may be an attempt, that's all. And the police, on whom you consider we should rely, think otherwise, or at least refuse to take the precautions I have asked for."

"I see," said Mr Gorringer gravely.

"Are you staying in the town?"

"I am. I have felt it my duty to be present here and perhaps—who knows?—lend some assistance, while taking every care that the name of the school shall not be involved in unwelcome publicity."

"Tired of Brighton?"

"As I explained to you the Sandringham Private Hotel is no longer in the capable hands of our good Mrs Tunney. I need not enlarge on the somewhat disagreeable incidents that have made our stay uncomfortable. Suffice it to say that we are spending a week here at Buddington before returning refreshed for the new term."

"In this hotel?"

"No, my dear Deene, not in this hotel. The Governing Body of the Queen's School, excellent in intention though they may be, do not see fit to increase my emoluments sufficiently to allow for luxury like this. We are staying at a small and I hope exclusive establishment named the Osborne. And now I shall be grateful if you will put me in the picture."

Carolus gave the headmaster an outline of the case and as he finished he saw Colonel Baxeter himself approaching from the entrance hall. He wore shorts and woollen stockings, an open khaki shirt and a jacket of grey homespun. Carolus quickly told the headmaster that he was 'connected with the case' and Mr Gorringer was a little more gracious than might have been expected considering the Colonel's attire. His rank also seemed to quieten the headmaster's alarm.

"You wanted to see me, Deene?" said Colonel Baxeter when introductions had been made.

"Yes. A few words with you and your wife, if I could."

"We are at your disposal. My wife has instructed me to invite you to share our lunch today and perhaps Mr Gorringer will join you?"

Carolus, who had dreaded a meal at Dehra Dun, now saw possibilities in the situation and Mr Gorringer, who knew nothing of the Colonel's rules of health, beamingly accepted.

The lunch was not a success. The headmaster, whose appetite was a healthy not to say voracious one, looked unhappily at the dish of various so-called 'edible seaweeds' which had been skilfully prepared.

"Slouk," said the Colonel, "excellent when dressed as this is with pepper and olive oil. Redware, you should squeeze a little lemon over that. Badderlocks which have also the pleasant name of Honeyware. They do not belie that name. Dulse you will find tastes like roasted oysters."

"Interesting," said Mr Gorringer without conviction. "And you feel no hardship in subsisting on these foods?"

"Hardship? You will find them delicious. We have a nut roast to follow with salsify and alecost."

Carolus turned the talk to murder, as a relief.

"I daresay I'm an alarmist," he said, "but I have an obstinate idea that there will be another attempt."

"Then you are coming round to my opinion that only a maniac can have been responsible?"

"I don't see why you should say that. What I want to

point out is that the only known link between the two persons murdered is that they both sold gold to Ebony. Far-fetched though it may seem, I think that may be the key once again."

"What does that entail? Are you seriously suggesting that anyone who has had dealings with this man is in danger?"

"I only know of two people," said Carolus evasively. "Mrs Bickley, the housekeeper at Rossetti Lodge, and Mrs Baxeter."

The Colonel and his wife exchanged glances.

"Do you mean us to take this seriously?" asked the Colonel.

"I do. Yes."

"Do you know that my wife represented this country at the Olympic games at Helsinki in 1952 and with the discus made Nina Romaschkova tremble for her title? That in the shot-put Galina Zybina acknowledged her prowess, while her javelin-throwing secured her congratulations from Dana Zatophkova of Czechoslovakia, who actually managed to win the event? Do you think she is a woman to be scared by some puny strangler?"

"A little more sea-girdle, Mr Gorringer?" said Mrs Baxeter, to deflect attention from her accomplishments.

"No, thank you!" said the headmaster with lively emphasis. "Health-giving, I make no doubt, but I have had sufficient."

"Anyway," said Carolus. "It seemed up to me to warn you."

The Colonel nodded.

"Your intentions are good," he said, "but we shall not change our time-table. This afternoon we are doing a cross-country run in the direction of Lilbourne and this evening we make one of our brief appearances at the Dragon. We occasionally visit it to avoid being considered exclusive or unsocial, unhealthy though the atmosphere undoubtedly

135

is. I think you would find that your murderer would find rather a warm reception at Dehra Dun."

Shivering before the open windows Carolus doubted it.

"My wife," went on the Colonel, "is a firm believer in peaceful relations between men as between nations."

"Satyagraha," put in Mrs Baxeter.

"But of course were she roused by any such attempt at violence her response would be instantaneous and effective."

In the car afterwards the headmaster looked pained.

"Salubrity, yes," he said. "Hygiene, dietetics, therapy, hydropathy within reason, all may have their place in our modern world. But sea-weed, my dear Deene, surely that is carrying vegetarianism to excess? And did I gather they were, hm, nudists?"

"You did. Both of them."

"I find the suggestion most distasteful. Where do our duties lie now?"

"There is not much more I can do."

"Tell me, for in this case the matter is surely too serious for deliberate mystification, do you know who murdered those two poor women?"

Years of habit made Carolus recoil from the question, but he recognized the truth of Mr Gorringer's remark.

"There are three persons," he said slowly, "any one of whom it could have been. You know the verse in Guy Mannering?

> *Gin by pailfuls, wine in rivers,*
> *Dash the window-glass to shivers!*
> *For three wild lads were we, brave boys,*
> *And three wild lads were we;*
> *Thou on the land, and I on the sand,*
> *And Jack on the gallows-tree!"*

"You mean that one of your three will hang?" suggested Mr Gorringer lucidly.

136

"I have every reason to hope so."

"I can scarcely suppose the Baxeters are among your suspects, then. There was little sign of 'gin in pailfuls' or any other of the boisterous features of your verse in their house. How, may I ask, do you intend to establish the identity of the murderer from among your three suspects?"

"Murderer or murderers," said Carolus. "I am awaiting a revelation."

"That sounds very obscure."

"Not at all. I have told you that I believe there will be another attempt."

"So some poor woman is to risk, perchance even to lose her life before you can bring the guilty to book?"

"I think I can eliminate the risk."

"Would it not be wiser to inform the police of your suspicions?"

"The police know as much as I do. They're not wasting their time, I assure you. They will almost certainly make an arrest before my case is complete."

"I devoutly trust so. You appear to me, my dear Deene, to be playing fast and loose with people's safety. What may be taking place at this moment in the seemingly placid town of Buddington? How can you be sure that even now your murderer is not preparing for his grim task? Or even executing it! I positively shudder at the thought."

"So do I. But I don't see what else is to be done. These murders were planned with diabolic forethought, care and precision. No old-fashioned 'clues' were left to help us, no bits of fluff or cigarette ash or fingerprints. In one case the person who dragged the body into a stone quarry took the precaution of wearing a stolen pair of shoes in order not to leave his or her own footprints. I have nothing but circumstantial evidence of the involvement of even the three and certainly nothing to incriminate one or another of them. I may guess, but so may you, and your guess is as good as mine. The only hope of deciding is to wait until there is another attempt. For that I am ready."

"What makes you so sure there will be another?"

"I am not sure. I have a strong feeling, that's all. If there isn't, I doubt if the case will ever be cleared up."

"Dear me. Your first failure."

"I think you should come back to the Royal Hydro for a cup of tea, headmaster. It is an illuminating spectacle to see the ailing rich enjoy their confectionery and you have not met the lady for whom, formally, I am acting."

"I should be happy. Who is this lady?"

"A Miss Tissot, unhappily, since she believes in 'the glory and the nothing of a name', christened Martha."

"Speaking of names, my dear Deene, Mrs Gorringer made one of her neater witticisms today. We expected to find you, after your illness and the anxieties of the case, worn to a shadow here in the country. 'The sly shade of a rural Deene', said Mrs Gorringer. I must say, I laughed heartily," said the headmaster and repeated that noisy performance in which Carolus tried feebly to join.

Miss Tissot received them without hostility. Mr Gorringer's sober and pompous manner seemed to satisfy her exacting standards. She swallowed hard on hearing his name, but bowed in answer to Carolus's request that they might join her. She was already enjoying mustard-and-cress sandwiches with the prospect of éclairs.

All might have gone well as Carolus gave her what information he thought proper and said that he hoped for elucidation soon. But unfortunately she looked up as Mr Gorringer was bowing to a group of people nearby.

"You *know* someone in this hotel?" she questioned incredulously.

"One of my Board of Governors," said the headmaster with undeniable pride. "Sir Willard Hoxton."

"You surely don't mean one of that group near the pillar?"

"Yes. That is Sir Willard."

"Confidence tricksters," said Miss Tissot. "The hotel's full of them since it began to go down."

"I beg your pardon," said the headmaster, colouring, "Sir Willard Hoxton is very far from being anything of the sort. A most distinguished gentleman with large interests in enamelware, I believe."

"Scum. Riff-raff. Rabble. Dregs," said Miss Tissot sweepingly. "I am surprised that you should acknowledge such rag-pickers when you are sitting with me."

The headmaster rose to his feet.

"In that case I can easily vacate my chair. The gentleman of whom you are speaking . . ."

"Gentleman? Vagabond. Guttersnipe. Pot-walloper. There are no gentlemen in this hotel. *Your* name sounds like a dress shop."

"And yours, Madam," thundered Mr Gorringer awefully as Miss Tissot attacked her *éclair*, "yours sounds like a sneeze."

He strode away, his face crimson but his carriage upright. Carolus smiled.

"You shouldn't take one another seriously," he said.

"Gorringer!" cried Miss Tissot. "I have never . . . Incredible . . . Thank heavens my stay here is nearly done."

A page-boy whispered to Carolus. A lady wanted to see him. The head porter thought it best to tell him so that he could come out. The head porter didn't think he would want the lady shown in.

By the desk, impatiently fingering her black kid gloves, was Mrs Gosport, whose lilies had been stolen before the murders. Her beady eyes were sparkling with excitement as she beckoned Carolus away from the hearing of those at the desk.

"You know what you told me?" she whispered.

It was not a fair question.

"I'm afraid I . . ."

"About my lilies. You said if any more of them was to be stolen to let you know."

Carolus at once looked serious.

"I remember."

"Well, they have. Or rather one has. And it looks like by the same person. Snipped off near the ground."

Carolus led her to a settee.

"When was this?"

Now that she could feel the full weight of importance in her information, Mrs Gosport was not going to be hurried. She licked her lips.

"Last night, it must have been, though I've only just noticed. You see they're over, really, the lilies. They can't go on for ever and I must say mine last longer than most. They were nearly done for though, with all this weather we've had. Just a few blooms on the turn. But I always let them die off naturally, because they're better for next year like that. I was only saying to my sister last night, the lilies are over for this year, I said, so we must wait till next when I hope no one will start cutting them again."

"You found . . ."

"It wasn't till this afternoon when I was pulling out a couple of weeds I happened to notice it. Just near where the others had gone, it was, and sliced off with a knife the same as they had been."

"But you think it was done yesterday evening?"

"I'm sure of it. I told you my sister was a ninvalide and she has her seat right in the window all day. It's something for her to do, poor soul, watch the people go by, because she can't do much in the way of needlework and she doesn't care for reading. So she has the radio on and looks out of the window, which I tell her is as good as the telly which we can't afford. So if anyone had come after those lilies in daylight she would have seen them, wouldn't she? That's why I say it must have been last night or the early morning."

"I see."

"Is it going to help you find out who got the other lot, because I'd like to know."

"I think it is."

"It's important, then? Not like all that about an artist ringing bells at Westmacott's. I thought, as soon as I saw it gone, this is important, I thought, and came running round at once."

"I think you should tell the police."

"No. They've never been to see me about the others. Why should I bother with them?"

"It's your duty, Mrs Gosport."

"Yes, and it was their duty to come and see me. If they had time to ask questions of Mrs Plummer till she went about telling everyone she was in with them and knew who had done the murders, they should have had time to come and see me. *You* can tell them, if you like. I shall leave them to find out."

"Would there have been any bloom on the one stolen?"

"Just a bit, I daresay. Oh yes, there'd be some bloom, only it would be going off on the edges, as they do. It would have kept better in water. I wonder he didn't take them all at the same time. Can you think why he didn't?"

"Yes."

"Why, then?"

"Because he, or she, or they, didn't know that a third one would be necessary."

"You don't mean someone else is going to be done for and found holding one of my lilies? If so, it's enough to put one off growing them."

"No one is going to be murdered if I can help it."

"Well, I hope you do, then, that's all I can say. We don't want some other poor lady found strangled and holding one of my lilies, do we?"

"No," said Carolus truthfully. "We don't."

15

CAROLUS went up to his room and rang for a waiter. When Napper appeared he sent him for a large whisky and a bottle of Schweppes.

"You look pretty grim," remarked Napper as he poured out the drink. "Anything wrong?"

"A great deal. I wish I had never gone near this case. It's going to end badly."

"Who for?"

Carolus ignored that.

"My trouble is," he confided to Napper, "that I appear to take things lightly and when I want people to understand that they are not an amusing game of cops and robbers they just smile and ask me what trick I'm going to pull out next. I honestly believe that at least one woman is in danger to-night and I doubt if I can convince the right people of it. It depends on such seemingly trivial things, a man buying old gold and the theft of a faded lily. Doesn't sound like another murder, does it?"

"I don't know. The lily does, rather. The point is, do you know who's going to be attacked?"

"I think so. But I can't be absolutely sure. It *could* be any elderly woman in Buddington who is alone this evening."

"Can't the police do anything?"

"Not much, can they? They can't provide a bodyguard for all the old women in the town."

"I see your problem. You'll obviously concentrate on the one you fear for most."

"I shall. But you can see how crazy it all sounds."

"Not more crazy than the murders themselves."

"Perhaps not. Only I feel responsible for the protection of certain people. Tell me how to get myself taken seriously, will you?"

"I don't think you need worry. You look pretty grey and serious now, if it's of any help to you. Anything more you want?"

"No. I'm going to lock this door for ten minutes, because I want to be undisturbed. Then I'll phone the police."

Carolus remained in a deep armchair, but he had not that yogi-like immobility that was his at times, for now he was not facing a problem so much as deciding on a course of action.

At last he rang John Moore. He spoke carefully and seriously.

"Look, John, another lily has been stolen from the front garden from which two were taken before the murders."

"Have you rung to tell me that?"

"Yes. It seems to me a very serious matter."

"You still believe another old woman is going to be attacked?"

"I do. I want to make you believe it."

"Who is it to be this time?"

"Almost certainly the Westmacotts' housekeeper, Mrs Bickley."

"What do you expect me to do about it?"

"Protect the woman."

"I could almost believe you are trying to make a fool of me."

"Someone is, John. Someone who went to enormous trouble and some risk to leave a lily on each of two corpses and has now stolen another. But there is a kind of fooling that is more deadly than the most solemn behaviour. Will you at least let me tell you what I want you to do?"

"Go ahead."

"I realize that you're in a difficult position. You've only just taken over here and all you've got to go on are my prognostications, which wouldn't convince any one of your superiors. So I won't ask impossibilities. But surely you can give your men a general alert? Something to the effect that there is reason to think that another murder may be attempted tonight? At least the suspects in this case, if any of them behaves in an odd way, may come under observation. It can't do any harm, surely?"

"I suppose not. In general terms like that. Anything else?"

"Yes. I want you, personally, to come with me to Bickley's cottage behind Rossetti Lodge and remain there for a couple of hours while Bickley shows himself in the Dragon. You can be off duty, surely, or else asking Mrs Bickley a few questions? You're not committing yourself."

"I could do that, but what good would it be? Do you think the murderer is going to walk in?"

"Yes, John, I do."

"I think you're barking, Carolus. I've always thought so. But I'll come."

"Good. Thank God you're in charge of this case instead of some moron who would already have made an arrest. Where can we meet?"

"Unobserved, you mean? I suppose your sense of melodrama demands that."

"I demand it, anyway. The Bickleys have their own little door in Orchard Street. We can get in that way without being seen."

"In that case I'll meet you outside the Windmill; that's a small pub on the corner of Orchard Street."

"At eight o'clock?"

"Yes. You're really in earnest, Carolus?"

"Dead earnest. I shall go now to the Dragon and remain there till I come to meet you. I want to see who shows up. And leaves. But I'll be at the Windmill on the dot. We might almost synchronize watches."

"If it would amuse you. It is six twenty-four."

Almost as soon as Carolus had put the receiver down the bell rang again. It was Mr Gorringer.

"I realize," he said, "that while you are engaged in work

144

of this kind you cannot be responsible for the behaviour of people you introduce to me. But really, Deene. Seaweed for lunch and at teatime the gross impertinence . . ."

"I can't really stop now," said Carolus. "I have to run."

"Whither, Deene? I have not come to Buddington for nothing. Pray tell me where you will be pursuing your enquiries this evening?"

"At the Dragon. If you like to come to the bar there in ten minutes you will find me. I shall . . ." At that point Carolus did what Ben Johnson had described as 'working the old receiver trick' on the headmaster and fled from the room.

But as he pulled up at the Dragon he saw a tall figure standing outside and in spite of the cap pulled over the eyes and the heavy muffler he recognized the headmaster.

"An adventure indeed," said Mr Gorringer. "I may say that I have not done what I believe is inelegantly called pub-crawling since my undergraduate days. I am relieved to see that you are not accompanied by the boy Priggley."

"No. Priggley has made himself scarce for the last day or two. I suppose he has found what he no less inelegantly calls 'a piece of homework'."

"You don't mean that the boy may have formed some undesirable liaison?"

"No reason to think that. He has taste of a sort. Let's go in."

Miss Shapely received them with regal geniality and poured their drinks herself.

"I forgot to mention," said Carolus aside to Mr Gorringer, "that you're a television photographer. Talk about the lighting, or something."

The first surprise of that extraordinary evening came when Thickett entered the bar. He was, of course, served by Fred. Carolus noticed that he was wearing what could only be described as a Sunday suit.

"He very rarely comes here," said Miss Shapely in answer to an enquiry when Thickett had taken his pint to a far corner. "I've no doubt he finds other places more suitable. Not that I've ever had any Trouble with him. He seems to behave himself."

There were other familiar faces. Charlie Carew was in conversation with Ben Johnson. They sat one on each side of a small table on which an aspidistra in a large pot irrelevantly flourished. At some distance from them Dan Westmacott and his wife sat with Raydell. Carolus nodded and smiled to them. Old Mr Sawyer was busy re-ordering. There were several rather nondescript strangers, but two customers whom Carolus hoped to see before he left the bar, notably the chauffeur Wright and the car-park attendant Gilling, had not yet appeared. Bickley, he knew, would not leave his wife.

Luck was with him in another respect, though. Or was it? The Baxeters paid one of their rare visits and came straight across to Carolus.

"I need scarcely say," the Colonel began, "that we drink nothing here but lemon juice. But my wife and I pay a visit occasionally for the sake of good fellowship. We do not wish it to be thought that our rational way of life makes us unsociable."

"We are quite gregarious, you see," added Mrs Baxeter.

Mr Gorringer, mellowed by a whisky-and-soda, became very courteous.

"I'm glad to have the opportunity," he said, "of thanking you again for that delic . . . er excel . . . that most interesting lunch."

"You like our simple fare? You should try my wife's mock pigeon pie. Made from aubergines and coco-butter," said the Colonel.

"And prunes," put in his wife.

"No doubt most health-giving. But we must not distract Deene. He has us all under observation, I suspect. Who,

146

may I ask, is that particularly loud-voiced individual in corduroys?"

"That's Ben Johnson, one of the best of the modern painters."

"The name is familiar to me," said Mr Gorringer unsmilingly. "Somewhat morbid subjects, I believe?"

"Writhing skeletons and death-watch beetles," said Carolus. "I think you said you knew him, Colonel?"

"I said I had met him once," said the Colonel bitterly. "He was an acquaintance of the late Miss Carew."

"And with him?" went on Mr Gorringer, who was enjoying himself.

"That's Charlie Carew, the nephew."

"Ah, the bar, I see, is a hotbed of suspects."

"Want some more?" said Carolus. "At the table behind you is sitting the elder son and heir of the other murdered woman. With him is his beautiful wife and a farmer who owns an ocelot."

"Dear me. A veritable detective's paradise. May I invite you all to join me in another glass? We will drink to a swift solution to this problem."

"Lemon juice," stipulated the Colonel.

"Did you not find, sir, that your rules of health were somewhat ill-attuned to a military life?"

"When I was in the Army," admitted Colonel Baxeter, "I had not yet met my wife. Naturism was still foreign to me."

"Ah. As well, perhaps," said Mr Gorringer genially.

Watching Miss Shapely, Carolus saw her face suddenly brighten.

"Well you *are* early tonight, Mr Gilling!" she exclaimed with scarcely disguised joy.

"I couldn't stand another minute of it," said the car-park attendant who had entered hurriedly. "My sciatica is playing me up something dreadful tonight and I'm more than half sure I've got appendicitis coming on. It seems to shoot right up and down my right side. I don't like giving in, because we ought to grin and bear it, oughtn't we? But with my catarrh as well I didn't feel I could stay over there another minute."

"There! What are you going to have?"

"There's only one thing'll do me any good and that's a drop of gin. I'd give my right hand for a nice light ale, but you know what it would do to me, don't you?"

"It's too bad," said Miss Shapely vaguely but fondly. "Try that and see if it picks you up a bit. You want looking after, that's what's wrong with you."

An argument seemed to have arisen between Charlie Carew and Ben Johnson, both of whom had been drinking somewhat heavily.

"All I said," Charlie Carew maintained, "was that there is a story going round that you were expected there that night."

"And I say I never had any intention of going near the place."

"All right. All right," said Charlie Carew. "No need to get excited."

"Do you think I'd have been to see that old bitch?"

"Mr Johnson," called Miss Shapely. "You know very well I won't have Language in my bar!"

"What language?"

"Beginning with B," explained Miss Shapely, drawing herself up sternly.

"There are lots of words beginning with B," said Ben Johnson and named two of them loudly and unforgivably.

"You will kindly finish your drink and leave, Mr Johnson. And don't come into my bar again."

Ben Johnson named two more.

"Fred!" called Miss Shapely menacingly.

But Ben Johnson, shouting the final and by far the most forcible word beginning with B, stumbled out. Charlie Carew laughed noisily.

"There is nothing to laugh at, Mr Carew," said Miss Shapely.

"He missed one!" said Charlie Carew. "What about bottom? Does it qualify?"

They never knew the answer, because Miss Shapely's attention was distracted by the entrance of the chauffeur Wright, with a shy-looking girl who seemed likely to be his 'young lady'.

In a few minutes Wright, having deposited the girl at the only table remaining unoccupied, approached Carolus.

"You'll excuse me, sir," he said somewhat smarmily, "but that's the man I told you about. Sitting alone by the door. The one who looked in the car windows, I mean. With the ginger moustache."

"Yes, I thought it was," said Carolus carelessly.

"What do you think I ought to do about it? My young lady's very upset."

"Nothing," said Carolus firmly. "She'll get over it."

Wright seemed dissatisfied, but slowly returned to his table.

"Mystery upon mystery," said Mr Gorringer, almost gleefully.

Soon afterwards the Baxeters prepared to leave. Mr Gorringer bowed gravely.

"Most enlightening," he said insincerely to Mrs Baxeter who had been talking about vegetarian cookery when the argument broke out. "I must suggest that my wife experiments with some of these salubrious dainties."

"Tell her to try nut fish," advised the Colonel. "Chopped pecan nuts and hominy, with breadcrumbs, walnuts, grated onion, hard-boiled eggs, all moulded to the shape of whatever fish you prefer."

"And chopped parsley," his wife reminded him.

"Sounds delec . . . appetiz . . . very nutritious," smiled Mr Gorringer.

"Are you going straight home?" asked Carolus casually.

The Colonel stared for a moment, then remembering the morning's conversation smiled broadly.

"I don't think you need feel any concern for my wife," he said and the two left the bar.

Carolus noticed that Thickett closely followed them.

It was now a quarter to eight and Carolus prepared to leave for his rendezvous with John Moore. He did not want Mr Gorringer to accompany him.

"Look, headmaster, I have to leave you for a time. I wonder if it would be possible for you to stay on here and make notes of one or two things for me?"

"Certainly, Deene. I have told you I am willing to lend my aid."

"What about your dinner?"

"I told Mrs Gorringer I might not be present for the evening meal, known as early supper at the Osborne. She most wittily misquoted Wordsworth in reply.

> *I take my little Gorringer*
> *And eat my supper there,*

she said. Now who is to be observed?"

"Shortly, I think, a man named Bickley will come in. He is a typical ex-policeman in appearance. I should like to know what time he comes and leaves."

"You shall," pronounced the headmaster.

"Then that group of Westmacott and his wife and Raydell. Also the man Gilling. It is possible that Ben Johnson or Thickett may return. But I would ask you particularly to notice Charlie Carew."

"You may rely on it, Deene. A novice in such things I may be, but long years of observing boys has taught me something. Anyone else?"

"The chauffeur who spoke to me, and the girl with him. That's all."

The headmaster was visibly preparing himself for the strain. His cap was pulled a little farther over his eyes and he took up a commanding but not brightly lit position at the end of the bar.

"It would indeed be a surprise to the many Old Boys and present boys, not to mention the Governors and staff of the Queen's School, Newminster, if they became aware that their headmaster had engaged himself in one of these criminological exercises of yours, Deene. It is scarcely in keeping with the position I occupy. *Quis custodiet ipsos custodes?* they might well ask one another in amazement. But since you assure me that the cause is worthy and may assist you in the detection of a murderer, I succumb."

"Thanks, headmaster."

"But I have your word, have I not, that neither my name nor yours will ever appear in any public account of this business?"

"You certainly have my word that I will do all I can to prevent it."

Just as he left them Carolus heard Miss Shapely address the headmaster.

"And what is your part in the programme?" she asked, with a queenly smile.

"Hm. Photography," said Mr Gorringer and screwed up his eyes as though measuring the volume of light.

16

CAROLUS had a strange feeling as he left the bar of the Dragon that it was for the last time, that he would not again see Miss Shapely ruling her domain with benevolent severity. He was very conscious of leaving behind him an atmosphere of warmth and light and good-fellowship, 'and laughter, and inn-fires', to come out into a night of darkness and driving rain with yellow street lamps making the buildings look drab and sickly.

He felt, too, that dull depression which so often settled on him as he neared the end of a case and saw the inevitable dénouement, the arrest and afterwards the long trial and the fearful punishment. He would not have it otherwise; there had only been one murderer in his experience whom he had wished to leave undetected, and that one was dead before he had identified her. Carolus was like all good sportsmen, he enjoyed the chase but not the kill.

He was convinced that tonight would bring the revelation he needed, but he felt no exhilaration. A human being, however guilty of whatever cowardly crime, putting his head into a noose is not an exhilarating sight.

Leaving his car outside the Dragon he started on the short walk towards Rossetti Lodge behind which was Orchard Street. The pavements were almost deserted and although as he crossed the Promenade he could see a few people round the Granodeon Cinema he passed only a policeman sheltering in a shop doorway.

But he turned once and saw at some distance behind him a man walking unsteadily in his direction. Charlie Carew, he decided, going according to custom to his home for food before returning to the Dragon for his last hour's drinking. Carolus decided to let him pass, and being just then near the house called Charlton in which Mrs Plummer was the caretaker he entered the gate and stood back. He did not need to be very cautious, for Charlie Carew lurched by, muttering, but Carolus thought he saw at one of the front windows of the house the moonlike shape of a pale face watching. Mrs Plummer, perhaps, was again worried about her dog.

Near the pub called the Windmill, John Moore was waiting. There was no greeting between the two men as they crossed the road towards the high wooden door beside the carriage doors of the stables of Rossetti Lodge. He rang a bell and after a few minutes Bickley called from the other side—"Who's that?"

John Moore told him and the wooden door opened, but Bickley bolted it again after they had passed through.

"Come in," he said, himself hurrying across the yard to his cottage, for it was still raining hard.

"Sorry to drag you out," said Moore when they had entered a comfortable sitting-room and removed their wet raincoats. "Mr Deene has something he wants to tell you."

"We were just looking at the telly," said Mrs Bickley, a little resentfully. "So please let's know what it is because I don't want to miss the next bit."

"I'm afraid this is rather serious," Carolus told them. "Another lily was stolen from the same garden last night. I believe that means that an attempt is to be made at another murder. As I have told you, I am convinced that the intended victim may be you, Mrs Bickley."

Husband and wife exchanged glances.

"I hope you're not upsetting my wife for nothing," said Bickley.

"I'm of course very sorry to have to come to you both with such an alarming story," said Carolus. "And I cannot pretend to be certain about it."

"What do *you* think about this, Inspector?" asked Bickley, with an air of speaking as one policeman to another.

"You put me in a difficult position," said Moore. "I am here quite unofficially, of course. At the same time I've known Mr Deene for some years and I have often found his ideas, though they seem far-fetched, hold water."

"I don't know what Inspector Wilkes would have said," remarked Bickley. "He was before your time and our Detective Inspector for twelve years. I can't see him running round at night saying someone was going to be murdered."

"No one is going to be murdered if we can help it," said

John Moore. "That's why we've come to you this evening."

"I want your help, Mr Bickley. I honestly believe that there's a good chance of clearing up this business for good if we act together."

"What do you want us to do?"

"I want you to go round to the Dragon and remain there till closing time. The Inspector and I will stay here with Mrs Bickley."

"Seems a funny business to me," said Bickley. "I don't know what Inspector Wilkes would have said."

"I'll give you my word, of course, that your wife will not be left alone till you return."

"You mean you think he'll come here? The one who murdered those two poor women?"

"I do."

"But whatever for?" asked Mrs Bickley. "Why should he want to do for me, I'd like to know? I've never done anyone any harm that I know of."

"Nor, I think, had Mrs Westmacott or Miss Carew. But they were strangled."

"If I really thought it was going to happen," said Mrs Bickley, "I'd like to have my husband here In Case."

Carolus found he had an unexpected ally. Perhaps Bickley wanted a drink.

"You'll be all right with them," he said. "Better off than with me, very likely."

"Still, it's not the same," said Mrs Bickley dubiously.

"He's a Detective Inspector after all," her husband pointed out. "And the other gentleman has helped in a good many cases."

"Why does he have to go?" asked Mrs Bickley.

John Moore answered.

"I don't know quite all Mr Deene's idea," he said, "but surely the murderer is scarcely likely to come here if he knows your husband's in the house."

"You think he's round at the Dragon, then?"

"Whoever and whatever the murderer is, I think your presence there, Mr Bickley, will be noticed," said Carolus.

"Don't forget there's several ways he can get in," Bickley pointed out. "He can't open the gates into Orchard Street, but on a night like this with no one about he could very soon hop over them, and there's a bit of wall there that a child could climb."

"Yes. I noticed it."

"I don't say he could get into this cottage, because the only windows look on to the yard. But he could come across from the house."

"So he could," said Mrs Bickley, "if he could get in there, and he seems to have managed that on the night he did for poor Mrs Westmacott."

"You needn't be uneasy, Mr Bickley. I assure you that neither Mr Deene nor I would take the slightest risk. We are not going to wait till he makes a move, if that's what you think. The mere fact that he comes here tonight will be sufficient for me."

"No, I'm not worried," said Bickley. "Nor's my wife, now she knows you're both going to be here."

"Well, I haven't been a policeman's wife all these years for nothing," said Mrs Bickley proudly. "I'll do it, so long as I can have the telly on. I'm not going to miss 'Blotto'. Not for any murderer."

Carolus writhed.

"I don't think the darkness . . ." he tried.

"You can lock the doors if you like," said Mrs Bickley. "But I won't be without seeing 'Blotto'. That's all about it."

"No one knows you're here, of course?" Bickley asked John Moore.

"I hope not. I'm pretty certain not, unless someone living in Orchard Street was watching."

"I think," said Carolus to Bickley, "it's time you went round to the Dragon."

"You'll want your umbrella," said Mrs Bickley. "It's pouring with rain and so dark you can't see your hand before your face."

When Bickley was ready Carolus came out to bolt the yard door behind him and returned to find the lights already lowered and Mrs Bickley squatting in an attentive posture before the television set.

"I've put the kettle on to make you a cup of tea," she said. "I'll go out when it boils."

John Moore sat where he could see the screen, but Carolus sank into an armchair on the other side of the room and closed his eyes.

He felt that he was facing his greatest test. He remembered how tenuous were the threads, what capricious assumptions he was making and how easily he could be altogether wrong, not in his interpretation of the crime itself—he was secure there—but in his prediction for this evening. He wondered whether he was not after all an interfering amateur.

John Moore showed extraordinary tolerance with him, he decided, but John Moore was an unusual policeman, and even he, quite rightly, had not committed himself to any official recognition of Carolus's scheme. He was here in a private capacity, about to have a cup of tea with an ex-policeman's wife.

"There!" exclaimed Mrs Bickley as 'Blotto' made way for the commercials. "Now I'll go and make your tea for you. I could do with a cup myself. It's the first time in my life I've ever had a murderer coming for me, so to speak, and I feel it, somehow."

"I'll come out with you," said Moore.

"Oh, there's no need for that. There's no back way into the house. Still, you can come if you like."

The two returned with the tray. Mrs Bickley hastened to

pour out and hand the cups, in order to turn down the lights again.

Time passed. Till a little past nine none of them moved, but then Carolus restlessly went across to the window.

"Can't see a thing," he said after peering out. "There doesn't appear to be a light in Rossetti Lodge either."

"Mr Gabriel's away a lot," said Mrs Bickley. "Goes up to London in his car. I shouldn't be surprised myself if he wasn't going to get married. I know there's Someone, because he's got the picture up in his room. Now hush, I want to hear this."

The only sound audible now was that of rasping voices from the television set.

In half an hour, thought Carolus, the Dragon will be closed and Bickley will return and any chance of the appearance he expected would be gone. But in the meantime, what? If the third lily had the significance he attributed to it, tonight was the last occasion on which he could reasonably expect results.

After another long silence he moved closer to John Moore.

"John," he said, "I've known you for a good many years and I've never been more glad of your British phlegm. You see, I happen to believe that an attempt at murder is going to be made now, in this town, within the hour."

"I know you do. I think you may well be right."

"Then how can you be so appallingly calm about it? After all, I've admitted that it's no more than a circumstantial guess of mine that it will happen *here*. I'm working on that because I can't do anything else. I can only be in one place. But you've got every old woman in the town as your responsibility."

Moore pulled at his pipe.

"The police can't be everywhere, either. In our clumsy way we have to get hold of the other end of the stick. The murderer's end."

"You mean you know who it is?"

"I'm at least as sure as you are about tonight. I can't provide every old woman in the town with a bodyguard. The best I can do is to have my suspects watched and followed."

"And you've done that?"

"Of course I have. You don't think I'd be sitting here if I hadn't?"

Carolus did not answer but Mrs Bickley spoke sharply.

"I wish you two would keep quiet for a minute. This is an interesting bit and all I can hear is murder, murder, murder, from the pair of you."

Once again time passed without an interruption. Carolus with difficulty looked at his watch and found it was nearly half-past nine. He began to be reconciled to a probable failure.

He heard the voices droning from the set and could distinguish the faint popping sound as Moore smoked his pipe. The room was close and drowsy.

Then, without anything to give warning of an approach, there were three loud hollow knocks on the door.

In these old converted stables there was no passage and the door behind Carolus opened straight on the yard. So within six feet of him, presumably, was standing the person who had given that melodramatic signal.

"What shall I do?" whispered Mrs Bickley.

Her hand went forward to switch off the television, but John Moore signalled her to leave it on. He took up his position against the wall to the left of the door while Carolus stood where the open door would shield him. The lights remained lowered.

"Get him inside," whispered Moore. "Whoever it is."

Before their preparations were fully made the knock was repeated, rather more loudly. The rain was probably still coming down and the visitor was impatient.

There was a chorus of inane laughter from the television set as Mrs Bickley went forward. Carolus remembered afterwards the glimpse he caught of the little woman, apprehensive and curious too, but courageous and determined. She pulled the bolt back.

As she opened the door the intruder pushed violently in. Mrs Bickley stood back and he almost passed her.

Carolus had his finger on the light switch and pressed it so that the intruder, as he came into the room, was brightly lit.

It was Gabriel Westmacott.

The first thing Carolus noticed about him was that in his right hand he clasped the stem of a lily, so faded and torn that it was scarcely recognizable. He looked like the crazy and degenerate caricature of a Pre-Raphaelite angel.

It was a pity, Carolus thought afterwards, that Westmacott became aware of John Moore's presence before he could speak to Mrs Bickley. It would have been interesting to know what those first words would have been. As it was he saw and recognized Moore. He did not look startled and guilty so much as angry. A hard, set expression came over his face, which was strangely white and wet from the rain. He spoke first.

"Where's Bickley?" he asked, presumably of Mrs Bickley, though he continued to look at Moore.

Years of habit made the little woman try to answer, though she was trembling now.

"He's . . . he gone . . ."

Westmacott turned to Moore.

"May I ask whether you are here in an official capacity?"

"Yes. You can call it that. I'm going to ask you to accompany me, Mr Westmacott. There are some questions I have to ask you."

"Accompany you? Where?"

"To the police station."

"Are you arresting me?"

"I am asking you to come with me and answer certain questions," said Moore stolidly.

Westmacott for the first time became aware of Carolus.

"Are you responsible for this, Deene?" he asked coldly.

"Well, in a way I am," said Carolus.

Westmacott seemed to be recovering his poise.

"Perhaps you were expecting me to come here?"

"Yes, I was."

"I'm sure it's all very clever, but I don't quite see what you hope to prove by it."

"Murder, Mr Westmacott," said Carolus quietly.

Gabriel Westmacott gave a short harsh laugh.

"Do you really?" he said. "How very interesting."

Mrs Bickley began quietly and as it were respectfully to weep.

"It's all right," Gabriel told her. "I shall be back in a few hours. They'll have to release me. This is simply a bluff without any proof behind it."

Mrs Bickley was concerned with other aspects of the thing.

"It's raining outside. You haven't got your coat. Take this old one of Bickley's."

"Thanks," said Westmacott coolly.

When he went to pull it on he became aware of the lily in his hand. For the first time he looked startled.

"This . . . this . . . I was just going . . ."

"Yes, Mr Westmacott?"

"I found . . . I was bringing . . . hell, I'm not going to discuss it now."

"Far best, because I'm just going to give you the usual warning. Anything you may say . . ."

The old rune came out, only remotely interrupted by some words of tense whispered dialogue from the television set.

17

CAROLUS was awakened next morning by the ringing of his bedside telephone. It was Mr Gorringer.

"A thousand congratulations, Deene. Buddington is ringing with your triumph."

"I don't feel very triumphant at this time of the morning," said Carolus.

"But you should. A veritable *chef d'oeuvre*. I little thought when you left me last night that it was in order to be present at the arrest."

"I wasn't sure myself."

"So skilfully yet so discreetly done that the police alone will publicly figure in the matter. I have already received an assurance from Detective Inspector Moore that your name need not appear. I could ask for nothing better. And now for your able analysis and exposition. When may we expect that? I am agog to know what led you through this labyrinth."

"Sooner the better."

"Then I shall take it upon myself to arrange the little audience which is so dear to you in these cases. Oh, I know you are entitled to your vanities. It will not be the first time that you have gathered the former suspects in a case, and all those who have been connected with it, and laid before them the facts. Who shall blame you for tasting that small triumph when the greater fruits of fame must be perforce denied to you?"

"It's really rather important in this case. There's a good deal yet to clear up."

"Say no more. It shall be arranged. If possible for today. My wife asks me to add her congratulations to my own. She says humorously that in future we shall have to change your title at Newminster to that of the Senior Mystery

Master. We shall meet anon, then, and I look forward to your elucidation of the problems which have exercised us."

Soon after this Priggley came into the room.

"Is this true?" he asked. "The floor waiter, whose incredible name is Napper, tells me that the police have got Gabriel Westmacott."

"That is so."

"So you've pulled it off again. Luck or deduction? Now, I suppose, you're pleased with yourself. But you're not going to pull the old gag of explaining the case to all the ex-suspects, are you?"

"Yes. I've got my reasons for it this time."

"But you *can't*, sir. It's positively nineteenth-century, that sort of thing. It belongs to the detective story world of growlers and deer-stalkers."

"The headmaster will arrange it."

"Oh, God! It's small wonder you're not among Julian Symons's hundred best detectives."

"If it's of any consolation to you it will be rather different this time. I've got to ask some questions as well as answer them. There's quite a lot I'm not clear about myself."

"Who will you question?"

"The headmaster, for one. Ben Johnson for another."

"Evasive again. When is this function to be?"

"This evening, probably. Meanwhile I shall stay in this room. I don't want to have to talk about the thing."

During the day Mr Gorringer kept in touch with Carolus. He seemed full of the importance of the occasion. He had found it possible to arrange for the 'little gathering' that same day and a room at the Royal Hydro, 'normally reserved for banquets' the headmaster explained, was to be, in his word, the *venue*. By lunch time Carolus knew that those described by Mr Gorringer as 'the principals' had accepted his ambiguous invitation, and Raydell was cooperating by bringing 'the Lilbourne contingent'.

"I think there will be no absentees from our muster," said

Mr Gorringer, "except, of course, that ill-mannered elderly woman who cast reflections on one of our Board of Governors."

"Miss Tissot? Won't she come?"

"I could not bring myself to ask her. If her presence is desirable that must be left to you. Colonel and Mrs Baxter will be there. I see no means of inducing the person who purchased gold to attend."

"No. I suppose not. That may be just as well. But Charles Carew? Gilling? Wright, the chauffeur?"

"All due. You will have no reason to complain of the size of your audience. I am allowing the boy Priggley to act as a messenger. Are there any others you particularly require?"

"Yes. Two women who will not be kept away when they hear of this, a Mrs Gosport and a Mrs Plummer." Carolus gave the addresses. "Then you say Raydell is bringing in Dante Westmacott and his wife? I hope he includes Mrs Goggs in his party and that you send Priggley for Thickett and, of course, the Bickleys. I'll phone John Moore."

He found Moore rather uncommunicative. Nothing was said about Gabriel Westmacott, but Moore agreed to come to the Royal Hydro at six.

"There's a small thing I want you to do for me, John. Arrange for a letter to be handed in to me a few minutes after I mention that it's coming."

"What letter?"

"Any letter. Addressed to me in typescript. Can it be done?"

"I suppose so. How you love your amateur theatricals, don't you?"

At lunch time Rupert Priggley gave him astonishing news. Miss Shapely would attend. She had informed Priggley that Carolus had been guilty of deceiving her, but in the circumstances she had forgiven him and arranged to leave her bar to Fred for an hour or so.

Carolus heard this without apparent interest.

"You seem frightfully blah about all this," said Rupert. "You're usually straining at the leash when it comes to the final disposal of evidence."

"I know. But this case is rather different."

"Expecting more fireworks?"

"I've told you there's a lot to clear up. I don't know quite how much."

"Well, don't produce any bangs. You'll upset Maurice Richardson. He calls you 'soothing'."

Carolus looked anything but soothing when he faced his heterogeneous audience at six o'clock that evening. He showed none of his flippant and easy-going manner, but appeared to be suffering from a strain of some kind. His face was set and rather drawn. Even the beaming pride with which Mr Gorringer greeted him failed to draw from Carolus a responsive smile, and he spoke to Mr Gorringer briefly and formally. He glanced for a moment at the small assembly as though to make sure that certain faces were among those present, then looked at his notes.

"To your text, Mr Deene," said Mrs Gorringer misquoting Queen Elizabeth I by only two vowels.

"One of the first things I realized about this case was that it was upside down. Usually the motive for a murder is clear enough and the investigator has the task of deciding who is to be considered a suspect. Here the suspects, several of them, were obvious enough, it was the motive which was baffling. What motive could there be for murdering *both* these women? If it had been possible to regard them as separate and unrelated crimes, it would have been easy enough. Several people had motives for murdering Miss Carew and several other people for murdering Mrs Westmacott. No one appeared to have a motive for murdering both.

"That, I saw at once, was the key to the whole thing. Find someone who would benefit by both deaths and all that would be necessary would be to dig up those bits of evidence which all murderers leave behind them.

"Detective Inspector John Moore, with far more experience and knowledge of criminals and their ways than I had, very wisely looked for a mercenary motive. For if there was a motive at all, if the murders were not the work of a homicidal maniac, it must be mercenary. Revenge, passion, jealousy, hatred, fear, all could be dismissed from any reasonable consideration. Yet here one was thwarted. Unless it was for a few hundred pounds believed to be missing from Mrs Westmacott's room, there had been no robbery and no one beneficiary was common to the two wills.

"So there we stuck and might remain stuck for ever if the murderer could not be induced by some means to reveal himself. It was most frustrating, because there was a singular lack of clues on which to attempt a more simple and practical solution. I saw no future in looking for fingerprints or footprints or those convenient little traces which are so often left. In any case I knew that if a conclusion was to be reached through these the police would reach it long before I should. They are experts in that field.

"Nor did I believe in the maniac theory. We know that a maniac may be enormously clever and cunning. We know that a homicidal maniac or a schizophrenic may pass for years as a normal person. But in this case I had reason to believe that the murders had been planned at least six months before they took place. There was a *kind* of calculation about them which was not the calculation of a madman. The very things that suggested madness, the lilies on the corpses and so on, were too deliberately bizarre to be credible as the work of a lunatic.

"Realizing that gave me my first illusory step forward. Whoever had murdered these women wanted his acts to appear those of a madman. He had gone to great lengths to achieve that. And great risks, too. Admittedly he had stolen the lilies before killing either of his victims so that if he were caught in the theft he would be guilty only of stealing flowers. Yet it was a risk and all for something which merely gave a macabre touch to the crimes. A madman might have thrown over a corpse any flowers found handy— only someone wanting to appear mad would prepare for the murder by stealing special flowers for it.

"Yet that still didn't show me his motive. I was still baffled by that and I had the feeling that I should never solve the case unless I could find it. I ask you, if you will, to consider that. You may have guessed long before yesterday who the murderer was, but it could be nothing more than a guess if you did not know his motive. Guessing is easy, particularly easy in this case, but it has got to be backed by something more cogent. So that although some of you may be congratulating yourselves on having guessed correctly, I say that you have no reason to do so unless you see why he did it. I believe there are only two people in the world who know that.

"It was a real puzzler and I almost gave it up. Mrs Westmacott and Miss Carew did not know one another, indeed had never met to our knowledge. There were certain tenuous links between them, but only such as must always exist between two residents in a small town like this. Both Mrs Westmacott's sons had met Miss Carew; both women had sold old gold to the same bullion dealer on the same day. But what significance could there be in that? It brought me no nearer to finding a common motive.

"I did not take seriously the possibility of the murders having been done by two different people working independently. It would mean the fantastic improbability that one of them stole a lily, murdered Miss Carew and disappeared for the rest of the evening while the other *chanced* to pass the stone quarry, *chanced* to enter it, *chanced* to find the corpse, and thereupon went off, stole another lily from the same garden and murdered Mrs Westmacott in the belief that whoever murdered Miss Carew would be blamed for it. That of course makes nonsense.

"Nor for a number of reasons which will emerge later, did I like the notion of two murderers working in co-operation. This is an old gambit and stories and films have been made from it. In this case it would mean that someone who might be suspected of wanting to kill Miss Carew but not Mrs Westmacott had made an agreement with someone who might arouse the opposite suspicions, and each had killed the other's victim, so that neither could be suspected of the murder he had committed. It sounds ingenious but it simply does not work out. In this case each would have made quite sure of an alibi for the murder of which he could be suspected and there was a notable absence of alibis among the suspects.

"I did find the motive eventually, otherwise we should not be here. But I am not sure that I can explain how I came to perceive it."

Carolus stopped and re-examined his notes. For the first time, when he looked up his face was less clouded.

"Let's have a drink," he said and called Napper, who had been put on duty for the occasion.

Conversation in the room was not animated at this point. As Mr Gorringer pointed out to Carolus, he had told them nothing yet.

"I have disposed of a few false trails, surely," said Carolus between sips of his customary whisky and soda.

"I told you my lilies would come into it," said Mrs Gosport loudly. "He's already been on about those and I haven't heard anything of anyone in a cloak calling at the house."

Mrs Plummer, sitting not far away, smiled, seeming to say that her time would come.

"Better bring another pair of those," Charlie Carew told

167

the waiter. "While we've got the chance. Don't you think so, Ben?"

Ben Johnson, beside him, nodded.

"Speed it up a bit," whispered Rupert Priggley to Carolus. "You're spinning it out like one of your history lessons. And what about the questions you were going to ask?"

Carolus ignored this. He had arranged that those present should be his guests this evening and was looking round to see that all who wanted a drink were supplied.

"Go and ask Thickett what he'll have," he said to Rupert, "and anyone else who hasn't got one."

"I trust this solicitude does not mean that we have some new shock to bear?" suggested Mr Gorringer jovially. "Ah, but I must ask no questions. Your health, Deene. We eagerly await some more substantive information."

But when Carolus resumed he seemed even less substantive.

"I am trying to explain," he said, "how I came to realize the murderer's motive. It did not come to me in the way fashionable among modern detectives, in a blinding flash of insight. But it did not come through reasoning, either. I think it was when I had reached the brick wall I have described. All possible theories seemed out. And suddenly, yes quite suddenly, I realized that I was thinking exactly as the murderer wanted me to.

"Now that was the point. The murderer had prepared for every eventuality, including investigation, both the expert investigation of the police and the more imaginative but probably less reliable kind of investigation of someone like myself. I was doing just what he wanted me to do—looking for someone with a motive for both murders and finding no one at all.

"Then I saw it. Whoever had murdered these two women had a motive for one murder and not for the other and by murdering both he had cleared himself of suspicion. You see the point? If he had only murdered the woman

168

he wanted dead he would have been discovered at once. At least he would have been identified at once and the evidence to incriminate him would almost surely have been found. But by gratuitously murdering the other he had covered himself. He had made the police and me and everyone else believe that either the murders were the work of a maniac or that someone must be found who had a motive for both. Ingenious? It was the most devilishly ingenious idea and it nearly came off."

John Moore sat staring fixedly at Carolus and unconsciously he slightly nodded his head.

18

"This discovery of mine, or if you like this notion, this probability, this theory, narrowed the field of suspects down to three. There were three people who had most evidently the traditional and sure essentials, Motive, Opportunity and Capacity, to do these two murders. I was irreverently reminded of the lines which I quoted to Mr Gorringer:

> . . . *Three wild lads were we;*
> *Thou on the land, and I on the sand,*
> *And Jack on the gallows-tree!*

"Now, since two of these who qualified as suspects are in this room I feel I must ask permission from you, Mr Carew, and you, Mr Westmacott, to talk as if you were not here. An explanation like this can be of no interest if it has to respect people's susceptibilities. I am sure you see the logic of that."

Charlie Carew, who had finished his pair of drinks, grinned beerily.

"I don't mind what you say," he agreed.

"Go on," said Dan Westmacott.

"Considering people we know as suspects must always seem somewhat fantastic, and murders like this in a small town in which people are known to one another, at least by repute, make it tough for the investigator. I do not mean that those three were the only possibilities, for Colonel Baxeter and Bickley could be said to have motives of a sort and their only alibis depended on the testimony of their wives, while even Wright had some kind of motive and nothing but the word of his fiancée to show that he could not have been at the two places at the relevant times. I also had to bear in mind the possibility that I was wrong in my analysis of motive, in which case others entered the field. But I decided to follow the theory I had formed and study the procedure of the murderer.

"I examined this in some detail.

"It was plain that he decided on his plan a considerable time ago, but like most clever murderers he avoided that greatest of all give-aways, hurry. A plan like this, though it might entail speedy action in its final execution, needed time to mature.

"He decided, I think early, that one of his two murders would be an outside affair, the other would be done indoors. How quickly he chose his victim for what I think we may call the false murder I do not know, but again I think some considerable time ago. He fixed the date only approximately, meaning to leave the choice of occasion to circumstances. The two deaths had to occur in a single night and be linked by similar methods and appearances if his plan was to succeed, for they must be seen to be the work of a single agency. It did not matter which he planned to make first, the true or the false, and he decided to kill Miss Carew before Mrs Westmacott.

"He had to find a place where the corpse would be discovered soon, but not too soon. It would never do for the corpse to be found before he had committed the second murder; on the other hand it must be discovered soon afterwards, or his plan would misfire badly and dangerously. So he hit on the quarry.

"But how was he to get Miss Carew out there? He was fortunate in that about this time an unlikely event took place—Mr Raydell acquired an ocelot and was indiscreet enough to take it into the bar of the Dragon."

"Indiscreet!" Miss Shapely could not help interrupting indignantly. "It was simply scandalous. Poor Mr Sawyer is upset every time he thinks of it. If ever such a thing should happen again . . ."

"Scarcely likely is it?" suggested Rupert Priggley. "There can't be a lot of ocelots."

"Priggley!" warned Mr Gorringer, and Carolus continued:

"Miss Carew was a lover of animals and as I heard from Colonel Baxeter frequently visited the Zoo. So when the evening came he could phone her (since he was acquainted with her) and suggest that they should run out to Lilbourne in her car and see the creature. He phoned from a call-box, as Colonel Baxeter observed, and while speaking to the Colonel disguised his voice. He made the arrangement, probably suggesting that Miss Carew should not tell her hosts at Dehra Dun lest they should wish to accompany her."

"A thing I should never have done," put in the Colonel. "My wife and I disapprove of keeping wild animals in captivity."

"Miss Carew was amused and pleased with the idea, but decided to phone Mr Raydell to confirm that he had no objection. We know of both ends of that conversation, for the Colonel remembered her shouting as if to someone deaf and Mr Raydell told me of Miss Lightfoot's reception of it.

"Our friend was picked up by Miss Carew at some appointed place where he would not be seen getting into the car on that dark night, and since she had as usual brought her Kerry Blue terrier Skylark and this dog, as Colonel Baxeter said, invariably sat in the front seat of the car, he was able to climb in behind without seeming to do anything unusual.

"On the way he asked her to stop for some reason, probably so that he could answer a call of nature, and when the car came to a halt he swiftly strangled her from behind, probably with her own scarf, perhaps with his. The dog did not realize what was happening and before he did anything else he chained the dog in the car. I imagine, since Miss Carew was going out to a farm, her dog would have a lead on him. Did you happen to notice that, Colonel Baxeter, when Miss Carew went out?"

"I did not, but it was invariable. Skylark was unaccustomed to traffic and never left the house, even for the car, unless on a lead—a thin chain it was."

"Thank you. So the dog was chained in the car and the body could be dragged across without interference. In the course of that Miss Carew's hat fell off and was found by Thickett next morning. What was more significant, perhaps, was that Mrs Goggs heard the dog barking furiously. It is a pity that she had not a clock, as then we should have known the time of the murder."

"You can't have everything," said Mrs Goggs sulkily, and no one ventured to dispute this profound truth.

"To return to our friend," said Carolus. "He had made two important pieces of preparation. He was possessed of a black cape and wide black hat, and wearing these and dark glasses, he had taken a pair of shoes to be repaired by a shoemaker called Humpling. While in his shop he had stolen a pair of shoes, but he was intelligent enough to choose shoes of his own size. Nothing could divert suspicion from him better than this, for he meant them to be found near the body. It would naturally be thought that the murderer was a man with much larger or much smaller feet, for who would trouble to steal shoes to leave footprints which might have been his own? This bothered me for a time, but I was beginning to get his measure and see the sort of bluff and double bluff he practised.

"The other thing he had done was, on the previous night, to steal from Mrs Gosport's garden two stems of Madonna lilies, one for each corpse. They were to indicate that one man was responsible for both and with any luck to suggest a homicidal maniac. There is something very odd about leaving those funereal flowers on a woman you have murdered. They achieved this very effectively. As they were found they were, we heard, somewhat crushed. That was to be expected, since he carried them in each case concealed under his coat. He left one on the corpse of Miss Carew and drove back to Buddington. His first murder was comfortably achieved and he had only to carry out the second, a far easier matter. He left the car in the car-park of the Granodeon Cinema with the dog still in it, and either during the night or while near the quarry the poor beast badly scratched at the upholstery in its efforts to get out.

"The hue and cry next day went exactly as he hoped. The corpse of Miss Carew was found almost at once, because Thickett was in the habit of leaving his road-mending tools concealed in the quarry. That of Mrs Westmacott was discovered by Mrs Bickley at almost the same time and the police found themselves with a baffling double murder and two stolen lily stems as almost their only clue. Days began to pass and our intelligent murderer saw his plan being beautifully justified by events.

"I felt myself rather ineffectual at that time. All I could do was to make routine enquiries. I found out a lot and as usual at such times a lot of scum comes to the surface. I found out that Wright, Miss Tissot's chauffeur, used his employer's car to take his respectable young lady out to a quiet spot on the Lilbourne road, where they doubtless held what I believe is called a . . ."

"Smooching session, I *hope* you mean," said Rupert Priggley.

"I also found that Thickett spent his evenings peering into cars parked by the roadside." Thickett seemed about to speak, but Carolus hurried on. "I heard the early history of Mrs Westmacott and her connection with the Pre-Raphaelite group of painters, and I heard a good deal about Mr Ben Johnson. I learnt of Miss Tissot's snobbishness, of a good many small and invidious differences between neighbours, of Gilling's ailments and Charlie Carew's Language, but nothing which would enable me to come nearer to a discovery of the murderer.

"I was convinced that the only hope of cornering him was to get him to break cover. It occurred to me that if he had committed one false murder to divert suspicion from himself, he might be made to feel it necessary to commit another and this time could be caught. If he was convinced that his plan had partly failed, that neither I nor the police thought the first two murders the work of a homicidal maniac, he might go out to make it more clear. Surely *three* dead women with lilies in their hands would be sufficient to convince the whole police force?

"I made a point of putting it about that the homicidal maniac theory did not hold water with me, and hinted that the police were doubtful about it, too. Meanwhile I persuaded Detective Inspector Moore, who was in charge of the case, to alert his men.

"At first I had no idea who the new victim was likely to be, but this became clear when I went up to town and saw Maurice Ebony. He lives by buying old gold by highly dubious methods, but he was as helpful as could be expected when it came to discussing these crimes. He told me that Buddington-on-the-Hill, once a paradise for gold-clappers in which almost every house had bits and pieces to sell, had

174

been so milked by his competitors that when he came here his very competent and attractive advance agent was scarcely able to obtain an opportunity for him. However, Colonel and Mrs Baxeter sold to him and recommended Miss Carew to do the same, and during the afternoon he went to Rossetti Lodge and bought from Mrs Westmacott. These were the only two buys he had on his first visit, but while at Westmacotts' he was told by Mrs Bickley that she had a few things to dispose of and on the day previous to my interview with him he had returned to Buddington and bought them.

"Now this was right up our murderer's street. He knew that those investigating had remarked on the fact that one of the few things connecting the two women was that they had both sold gold to Ebony, and he knew, as I very soon discovered, that Mrs Bickley made a third who had sold gold. It must have been irresistible to him."

"How did he know that?" asked Ben Johnson who was now taking an interest in the thing.

"Bickley made no secret of it. In his own words he 'told them in the Dragon' about it. But Mrs Bickley actually mentioned it to Gabriel Westmacott, as well as to Mrs Plummer and Grace Lightfoot. It was common knowledge. It made the choice of victim too easy. I became convinced that if there was an attempt at another murder Mrs Bickley would be the victim.

"What convinced me that it was coming was that Mrs Gosport had another of her lilies stolen."

"There! What did I tell you?" asked Mrs Gosport of no one in particular.

"It had been cut, she said, exactly as the others had, near the ground. I think it was a reasonable assumption that it was to be used for the same purpose. As soon as I heard of it I informed the police and we prepared for what seemed to me inevitable."

Mr Gorringer raised his hand.

"Since you are coming to the very climax, my dear Deene, to the story of your exciting vigil and the arrest which rewarded your efforts, I suggest a few moments' break. I know full well from my experience of lecturing how tiring can be the dissemination of one's own ideas. Let us relax for a while."

"Best idea this evening," said Charlie Carew. "What's yours, Ben?"

But Johnson seemed absent and pensive.

Beside Miss Shapely sat the respectable Mr Gilling, suitably solemn as he ordered gin and water, the only thing he dared touch, while Miss Shapely herself drank Port. The conversation between them was not intimate.

"Terrible thing," reflected Mr Gilling.

"But you could See it, couldn't you? I never thought he was to be trusted. Though I must say on the few occasions he has come to my bar he has known how to behave himself."

"Well, you wouldn't expect him to start strangling people there, would you?"

"I should hope not," said Miss Shapely with *hauteur*.

"Evening, Gilling," said Mr Raydell, "how's your duodenal ulcer this evening?"

Gilling stared.

"I haven't got a duodenal ulcer," he said.

"Haven't you? Too bad. They're easy to get, too."

"Very rude," said Miss Shapely to Gilling. "I don't know what's come over Mr Raydell lately. He used to be so quiet."

Colonel Baxeter leaned across to Carolus.

"Are we likely to be much longer, Deene? My wife and I find this atmosphere suffocating. Positively suffocating."

"I hope they don't start taking their clothes off here," whispered Mrs Plummer to Mrs Bickley, who sat beside her. "That *would* be a nice turn-out, wouldn't it?"

Mr Gorringer answered the Colonel.

"Deene is nearing the end, you will find. He has but to describe the final scene and our curiosity will be wholly satisfied."

"Our lungs, meanwhile, will have absorbed quantities of this foul air," grumbled the Colonel.

Carolus resumed.

"Perhaps you will think that I was assuming too much when I persuaded Detective Inspector Moore to accompany me to Bickley's cottage that evening. He came because we are old friends but not in his official capacity, for quite rightly he suspects the theories of amateurs like me. I admit I had not much to go on of a nature to appeal to him. Police methods leave nothing to guesswork or theorizing and not much, I sometimes tell him, to imagination. In this case he was right to be sceptical, I daresay, but all my instincts told me that it would be worth while.

"You see, I had come to know the mentality of this murderer. I had seen it at work in a dozen ways, I had, as it were, watched him from the first. I knew why he had killed two women and was almost sure that I had driven him to attempt to kill a third. If he had achieved it and remained undetected in that third crime he would have been free for ever. No one would believe that greed for one woman's money had been the sole motive for the murder of three. I shouldn't have believed it myself if I had come first to the case then. I had nearly been fooled by one false murder.

"The weakness of my position lay not in that I anticipated a new attempt but in being so specific about it. I believed it would come last night because the lily had been stolen the night before and would not even look like a lily much longer. And I believed Mrs Bickley would be the victim because I was sure that the man I had studied, whose thoughts I knew, would not miss that chance to give a further bewilderment to his pursuers.

"I persuaded Bickley to show himself in the Dragon. The murderer would clearly want to know that he was out of the way before coming to the house and would find out that he was in Miss Shapely's bar.

"Then we waited and, as you all know, it happened. At about twenty-five to ten there was a knock on the door and when Mrs Bickley opened it Gabriel Westmacott burst in. He was actually carrying the lily."

"So you were justified by events, eh, Deene?" said Mr Gorringer. "Your doubts and speculations were resolved. You had the satisfaction of seeing the fly walk into the spider's parlour, actually carrying the evidence of his guilt. As I have said, a triumph."

"It would have been," said Carolus ruefully. "If it had been the murderer."

"I beg your pardon?"

"Oh, but surely. You didn't suppose Gabriel Westmacott murdered his mother, did you? That would be too monstrous. Mind you, his night under interrogation will have done him no harm. His is not a pleasant character, but as for strangling two women, he hasn't it in him. Stealing from his mother's bedroom the sum of money she kept there in cash was about his mark. Not murder."

"Then who . . . why . . . I confess I am baffled," said Mr Gorringer.

"It was perfectly obvious," said Rupert Priggley, "that you didn't think Gabriel guilty or you would have used his name instead of all those coy references to 'him' and 'the murderer'."

"But I never dreamt . . ." admitted Mr Gorringer.

"Let's hear the rest of this," said Ben Johnson gruffly.

"All right, but we shall have to go back a bit. To the cloak with which there was no dagger. Didn't you all seize on that cloak? Such an outlandish garment. I should have thought you would realize that it was the clue to the whole thing."

19

"SIX months ago a man wearing a cloak, a wide black hat and sun glasses went to Mr Humpling's shop and stole a pair of shoes which, one may reasonably assume, were those found near the corpse. On the night of the murder Mrs Plummer, who is caretaker of the house opposite Rossetti Lodge, saw a man wearing the same things go up the steps of the house in which Mrs Westmacott was then alone. Co-incidence? Hardly. When I knew who that man was I knew my murderer.

"How was the murderer admitted to Rossetti Lodge? Only two people besides Mrs Westmacott had keys, her two sons. If it was one of these he would scarcely wear this melodramatic disguise to go to his own house. Yet the murderer was admitted and it can only have been by Mrs Westmacott herself. What on earth can have induced an old lady approaching eighty years of age, alone in a big house, to admit a man at nearly eleven o'clock? The answer is that she was expecting him and was delighted that he was coming. She was waiting for Ben Johnson."

A murmur went through the room, but Johnson himself did not change the fixed expression on his face.

"We know that for a long time she had wanted to meet Ben Johnson, to add him to her collection of artists, and he had steadily and sometimes rudely refused to have anything to do with her. That night she was to see him for the first time."

Mr Gorringer cleared his throat.

"I cannot help but interrupt," he announced. "What possible motive could Mr Johnson have for killing Mrs Westmacott?"

"None, of course. He did not kill her. I said she was waiting for him. She even phoned to remind him; he rather brusquely cut her off but unfortunately in a way which told her nothing. He was astonished that she should have phoned. Ben Johnson's name was the murderer's Open Sesame to Rossetti Lodge. It was easy to persuade Mrs Westmacott to receive *him*, and as she had never set eyes on Ben Johnson it was easy for the murderer, arriving in a cloak and hat such as artists wore in Mrs Westmacott's young days, to make her believe that he was Ben Johnson who had already phoned and that he wanted to paint her portrait. She did not know that Ben Johnson affected a different kind of artist's garb—corduroys and neckerchief. Coming from his success out at the quarry, the lily under his coat, the murderer entered quite easily and was soon chatting to his delighted hostess about her portrait.

"Do you think that odd? Do you think he was stretching it when he told an old lady of that age that he wanted to paint her? I don't think so. She had sat to painters for most of her life and was still a fine upstanding woman. Among other valuable things that Miss Lightfoot said to me was this: 'Supposed to be beautiful, she was. Just right for pictures of the saints. She wouldn't have done for it lately, would she? Though you couldn't tell her that. She still thought she ought to be in a stained glass window. Nearly eighty and expected to look like someone with a halo on.' No, I don't think there was much difficulty about persuading her to be painted.

"So all the murderer had to do was to go behind the couch on which she was sitting, with the excuse that he wanted to arrange a sort of halo of stars in her hair. From that position he could strangle her as silently and quickly as he had strangled Sophia Carew two hours earlier. Well, though I know his state of mind I cannot guess whether he left the trinket there on purpose or forgot it.

'I noticed there was a large mirror on the wall in front of the couch and it struck me as rather horrible that Mrs Westmacott should have been looking in it when she was strangled. The murderer showed her his little crown of stars, asked permission to adjust it, stepped behind the couch, and when he produced a scarf for a moment, the vital moment, Mrs Westmacott thought it was for her to wear when she was painted. Before she realized the truth or could raise any alarm it was already too tightly about her neck.

"The murderer was pretty sure of being alone in the house with Mrs Westmacott, for, as Miss Shapely told me, an announcement was published in the *Buddington Courier* that Gabriel Westmacott would be lecturing in Lancashire that evening. 'We all read that,' said Miss Shapely. 'All my regulars. It was handed round.' As it happened the paragraph was inaccurate and had been inserted by Gabriel himself to deceive his mother. He had as we know made an unexpected visit and had left only an hour before the murderer arrived at Rossetti Lodge so that it was only by chance that the murderer did not find him there. But he did not know that. The Bickleys could be relied on to be huddled and straining before a television set.

"I had, then, the *how*, the *why*, the *when* and the *where* of the two murders; what remained was the *who*, and I began to work towards identification by a process I often use. One might call it elimination. I put down all the things I knew about X and tried to see who fitted the role. When I say 'knew' I do not mean in the way the police have to know before they can make a charge, the way a court of law expects them to know, but in the way a lucky freelance knows. This was what I knew:

1. He was a man, not a woman or a collaboration or anything of the sort, but a man acting alone.
2. He would benefit, directly or indirectly, from one of the two wills.
3. He was known to Miss Carew, unknown to Mrs Westmacott, and probably unknown to Humpling.

4. He could drive a car.

5. He had the physical strength to strangle Miss Carew, drag her body some yards, and strangle Mrs Westmacott, all within three hours.

6. He possessed a black cloak and a wide-brimmed black hat.

7. He lived in the district and knew a great deal about its inhabitants.

8. He had no satisfactory alibi for either of the two occasions.

9. He was probably known to Colonel Baxeter, since he had disguised his voice to him on the telephone.

10. He was in urgent need of money, since he was prepared to murder an elderly woman in order to anticipate his own benefit from her death.

11. He knew enough about art to convince an old lady that he was an artist.

12. He knew of Raydell's ocelot, Gabriel's supposed absence to give a lecture, Mrs Westmacott's unsuccessful efforts to meet Ben Johnson, Mrs Gosport's lilies. Miss Carew's fondness for animals, Gilling's habits and the pedestrian's back way out of the Granodeon car-park.

13. He was not particularly tall or short. The only person to have seen him to my knowledge was Mrs Plummer. I made a point of *not* asking her about this, because my experience of too-willing witnesses is that if you suggest one or the other they immediately remember that the subject is very tall or undersized. But she would have mentioned it herself if he had been either.

14. He knew the Lilbourne road.

15. He made a call from a public telephone that evening and another call either from the same or from a private phone.

16. His absence till past twelve that evening was not noticeable.

"But when I had all these down and ran over them with the persons who could still be called suspects, I found that there were at least two of them who fitted, after a fashion, into all of them. So I could still make no final identification, though I knew, to my own satisfaction, who was guilty. Indeed, it is not till tonight, it will not be for a few moments yet, that I can name my man."

"A few minutes?" repeated the headmaster sternly. "What rigmarole is this, Deene?"

"While we have been sitting here, enjoying a drink and a chat, I hope, certain premises have been most thoroughly searched. You see, knowing my man's mentality I believed that though he could work out this elaborate and bewildering scheme of murder, he would make the usual slip, or keep something that would give him away, which would make him, in a word, that Jack on the gallows tree whom we want. I cannot hope to find anything as incriminating as the cloak and hat, but some little thing there will be, like the coil of thin wire from which some has been taken to make Mrs Westmacott's tiara or perhaps even some more starry spangles like those used. No, don't move, Carew. The information will be here in a moment."

"I'm not going to listen to any more of this ——" said Charlie Carew.

"Oh Mr Carew, your Language!" exclaimed Miss Shapely. "And beginning with B, too!"

"You have all thought I have dawdled over my explanation, and to tell the truth I have. I wanted to leave plenty of time for the search. But I assure you that the results will be here in a moment."

"Have those carrying out this search got a search warrant?" asked Colonel Baxeter.

"Surely you must know that recent cases have shown that the search warrant is regarded by the police as a complete anachronism, Colonel? A Home Secretary, since raised to the Peerage, defended their action in searching without a warrant on the grounds that it was customary. What more do we want? Ah, here are the results."

Carolus took an envelope from a man who had entered, ripped it open and read.

"We are more fortunate than I thought," he announced. "These most cowardly murders will be avenged and I use the word deliberately, believing as I do that society should avenge itself on those who commit deliberate pre-meditated and brutally cold-blooded crimes of this sort.

"But first let me clear up a small point which is worrying me and perhaps the more observant of you. How did that lily last night come into the hands of Gabriel Westmacott? He said that he *found* it. I wonder whether Mrs Plummer can help us here. Did you happen to notice anyone going to Rossetti Lodge last night?"

"Well, I was just letting the dog out . . ."

"Of course."

"When I *did* see someone go up the steps. It was before Mr Gabriel got back. I think he pushed something through the letter box though I couldn't see what."

"But you saw who it was?"

"I shouldn't want to say anything to get anyone into trouble . . ."

"You needn't worry about that. After what has been found in the search tonight nothing you say will make the case much stronger."

"Well, it was Mr Carew."

"That's a foolish lie. I was too tight last night to find the way to Rossetti Lodge if I had wanted."

"Were you, Carew?" asked Carolus whipping round on him. "Did you find him drunk, Mr Johnson, when you were together at the Dragon?"

"Yes. Pretty drunk. He drank a great many rums and kept pointing at things."

"Pointing? What sort of things?"

"I don't know. Shapely's shape . . ."

"Really, Mr Johnson!"

"Or a picture on the wall, or something."

"And did you look when he pointed?"

"I suppose so. Can't help it if someone points, can you?"

"That is why the earth in the aspidistra pot on your table has been found to contain the alcohol Carew ordered and did not drink. I knew he was acting when he followed me out of the Dragon, lurching all over the path. No, he was very far from drunk. He was shrewd enough to guess that a trap was laid for him at Bickley's. He had to do something with the lily and thought it must serve his purpose as well if he made it a sort of death warning."

Charlie Carew began to chuckle, apparently with good humour.

"How well he fits all my conditions," said Carolus. "But it was the black hat and cloak which gave me my first idea. For except from a theatrical costumier, where could you obtain such things unless your father had been, in Miss Tissot's words, 'an artist of the old and most disreputable school. A Bohemian, a vagabond, a character from the Latin Quarter who looked the part'.

"How easy was it for him to phone Miss Carew that night, disguising his voice from Colonel Baxeter, how easy to persuade her to drive him out to Lilbourne to see Raydell's ocelot, whose previous appearance in the Dragon bar he had witnessed. How natural that he who knew both Sophia Carew and her dog so well should volunteer to sit behind and leave Skylark his usual place. How easy to get Miss Carew to stop by the quarry which he knew from his cycling days. Then, when his task was done, how easy to leave the car in the car-park with the poor dog in it, having made sure that Gilling was over at the Dragon. Then he could leave the car-park by the back way and show himself in the bar till ten o'clock.

"Who was more likely to be in urgent need of money than Carew?"

"Who indeed?" grinned Charlie. "Will you ever stop talking, Deene?"

"When you begin. But all this would be merely circumstantial. It is true that an important piece of direct evidence has been provided by Mrs Plummer." Carolus caught an ugly look from Mrs Gosport and hastily adjusted matters. "She saw Carew and no one else pushing Mrs Gosport's lily through the letter box of Rossetti Lodge."

"Well, I don't know what to say," admitted Mrs Gosport generously.

"No more do I," was Mrs Plummer's olive branch.

"But even that is far from final. What is going to hang you, Carew, is the successful search of your house."

"Really?" said Charlie Carew.

Only Carolus noticed that his right hand was held palm upward in front of him.

"Stop him!" shouted Carolus.

But his open hand with its deadly little white burden had shot up to his mouth. Johnson, trying to hold it, was too late and they saw the movement of Carew's adam's apple as he swallowed.

It was some time after the reassembly of the Queen's School, Newminster, that the last word was said and the last explanation given of the murders at Buddington-on-the-Hill. At first Mr Gorringer seemed too busy to reflect on his remarkable experience of the holidays, and when at last he ventured to refer to it in conversation with Carolus it was only after a roundabout start.

Carolus had been watching the first school cricket match of the summer term and was about to make his way towards the school buildings from the pleasant little elm-surrounded ground behind them. Cricket and a June afternoon have their own peace and Carolus was enjoying it when he saw

Mr Gorringer bearing down on him, resplendent in a boater with some immensely significant colours in its hatband.

"Ah, Deene," he said. "A truly magnificent day. I see our excellent matron, Miss Pink,* has honoured us this afternoon. Mrs Gorringer made one of her aptest *mots* at her expense this morning. I had permitted myself to account for a vagary of Miss Pink's by speaking of the child in her, for there is a little of the child in each of us, Deene. 'The young person in Pink!' said Mrs Gorringer and I must say I could not restrain my laughter."

"No?"

"You, however, seem particularly unmirthful this term, Deene. Not dwelling on the unhappy events at Buddington, I trust?"

"Oh no."

"There are one or two things I have long meant to ask you about that. What, in fact, had the police found so incriminating in Carew's house when you received that note?"

"Nothing. They hadn't searched it. Even the police would scarcely break into a house and search it before they had arrested its occupant."

"A bluff, eh?"

"Yes. But backed by sense and reasoning. I was sure there would be something there, but even if there hadn't been Carew would suppose there was. As a matter of fact they found just what I suggested, a coil of the wire from which the so-called crown or tiara had been made. The cloak and hat have never appeared. He must have burnt them. But his wife (who was separated from him) remembers him having the articles and saying they had belonged to his father."

"Interesting," said Mr Gorringer.

"I was also bluffing about the aspidistra pot, but it was the obvious place for him to pour the rum he didn't drink. I never bothered to ask Moore whether I was right."

* See *Our Jubilee is Death* by Leo Bruce (Peter Davies).

"Perhaps, Deene, you may have realized that I guessed the murderer's identity some time before you revealed it?"

"That, headmaster, I must dispute, except in a limited sense. Like a man trying to pick a winner and going over the horses in a race, you may have dwelt on the name with others several times. But when that man has backed another horse, of whichever wins he says 'I *knew* that was the one!' Besides in this case it was no good just guessing Carew if you couldn't see why he murdered both those old women."

"These are mysteries," said the headmaster sonorously. "Was it ever discovered why Gabriel Westmacott had the lily in his hand when he came across to Bickley's cottage?"

"Rather natural, wasn't it? It was a disturbing thing, in the circumstances, to find in his letter box, and he came to consult Bickley about it. Moore knew that was his explanation, but could not, of course, give information from a man's statement to the police."

"Have you heard from Moore? He has surely expressed his gratitude?"

"Why? Carew was his suspect from the first. But he has written and told me of a forthcoming wedding."

"The young chauffeur's, no doubt?"

"That's broken off. Her parents were too respectable to allow their daughter to marry a man concerned in a murder enquiry. No—Gilling is to marry Miss Shapely. I understand that she will not, however, give up her bar."

"News indeed," commented Mr Gorringer. "There is one other point I should like elucidated. When I arrived at Buddington and you gave me a *resumé* of events, you laid great stress on the fact that there were *three* blooms on the lily stems and *seven* ornaments in the crown. Were you merely mystifying me?"

"Not in the least. Oh, well hit! Priggley is really quite a useful bat when he pleases. No, I wasn't being mysterious. That was a piece of business by Carew, clever in a nasty and perhaps rather blasphemous way. Knowing Mrs Westmacott's story, he suggested painting her as Dante Gabriel Rossetti's Blessed Damozel. You know—

> *She had three lilies in her hand,*
> *And the stars in her hair were seven."*

"I find that in excessively bad taste," said Mr Gorringer in a harsh voice.

"The whole thing was," replied Carolus and walked away.

THE END